MW01675412

JONAH

SUSIE MCIVER

BAND OF NAVY SEALS

BOOK 6

JONAH

AUTHOR
SUSIE MCIVER

This is a work of fiction. Names, Characters, organizations, places, events, and incidents are either products of the author's imagination or are used fictitiously.

Text copyright 2021 Susie McIver

All rights reserved.

No part of this book may be reproduced, or stored in a retrieval system, or transmitted in any form or by any means, electronic, mechanical, photocopying, recording or otherwise, without express written permission of the author.

Cover Design by Emmy Ellis

Created with Vellum

1

JONAH

Jonah could only stare at the beautiful Scottish beauty and wonder how Rory Walsh could get into so much damn trouble. First, he had to bail her out of jail because she attacked a guy she saw hitting a kid in the park. Jonah knew he would have smashed in the guy's face as well. The man was arrested, but Rory was so angry that the police thought she was drunk and arrested her. All because her Scottish accent got thick from all the emotions she was feeling. They couldn't understand what Rory was saying. After all, she had just seen a man hitting a child. That was reason enough to make her angry. The police hauled her off to jail for being drunk in public and starting a fight. Now the judge said if she didn't stay out of trouble, he would lock her up. That was last week.

Rory went to a club the other night and got into a fight with two women who made fun of her speech. Rory was a martial arts expert and had numerous belts to prove it. But she needed to stay out of trouble while she was in the United States.

"What caused the fight in the club?" the judge asked. He

held up his hand when Jonah was going to answer. "I want to hear from Miss Walsh."

"It's not my fault, your Majesty."

Jonah chuckled and shook his head, "It's your honor," he whispered.

"Your honor, I mean. The lasses were making fun of me and my country. They started the confrontation. What was I supposed to do?"

"You could have just walked away."

"I walked away and they followed me. When the one with the light-colored hair pulled my hair, I had to protect myself. I didn't hurt the lasses much, even though I could have. They obviously had too many drinks and the alcohol caused them to be rude, and mean."

The judge let her off this time. Jonah thought it was because he was under her spell. Like most of the males who talked to her. Jonah thought Kane should send her back to Scotland, where her sister was. But Rory thought Kane needed her here with him.

The woman was absolutely drop-dead gorgeous. She oozed sex appeal. Rory Walsh was all curves. Jonah preferred women with curves. She had black hair cut short, and it all curled around her head perfectly. Her eyes were as green as emeralds. Some people might call them bedroom eyes. Jonah tried not to think of those beautiful eyes and bedrooms together in the same sentence. He figured it might get him in a lot of trouble with her brother Kane because it would make his thoughts go to off-limit places.

Rory didn't like being in the city. She missed the green hills of Scotland. She told anyone who asked her how she liked living in the States. She thought there was too much cement.

"Rory, why do you go to the clubs by yourself?" Jonah asked, looking at her. Damn, she smelled good.

"Because I don't have anyone to go with. I enjoy being around happy people. Missy is so busy, and Dakota always has something going on. So I have to go on my own. I can't stay cooped up, I will go crazy."

"Understood, but it's pointless going out to be with 'happy people' if you end up in fights, isn't it?"

She nodded, agreeing with his point. "Well, no need to worry anymore, I'm starting work on Monday so I won't have time to be out here getting into trouble."

Jonah smiled inside, feeling only gratitude. Anything to keep her out of the courtroom. She won't be so lucky all the time. "Where are you going to work?" Jonah asked, surprised.

"A mental behavioral center in the city. It's a prison for unstable men."

"Interesting, and what will you be doing there?"

"I'm a psychiatric behavioral therapist."

"What? I didn't know that. Why didn't I know that?"

"You never asked. Did you think all I did was work on the farm?"

"Yes, that is exactly what I thought," Jonah admitted. He started to panic immediately, this was not a job he wanted to see her doing. Thinking of her as a farm girl was a much better, safer thought. "I don't think it's a good idea for you to work there. I know people in those places. They're locked up there for a reason. Most of those men will kill you for no reason," his thoughts were coming out quick and he couldn't see the annoyance on her face. Who was he to decide what kind of work was good for her? "You are not going to be in the same room with them, are you?"

"How else will I help them if I'm not in the same room with them?"

"You can talk with them on the other side of a divider. Does Kane know about this?"

"He's the one who told me to get a job. Because I need something to do. I'm used to staying busy."

"Why can't you work with Missy? She's always hiring people."

"I went to college a lot of years for my degree. I'm not going to work for my friend. How do you know about the people in these places?"

"I'm a lawyer. I put some of those people away. I know how they are."

"So do I. Don't worry, I'll be careful. I know how to speak to people with mental issues. I'm going to be there to help them, and they know that. I won't be harmed. You don't need to worry about me. I won't tell any of them I know you." She chuckled when he rolled his eyes.

RORY LOVED LISTENING to Jonah talk. She thought he was the hottest guy she has ever talked to. Sure all the Band members are handsome, but it was Jonah she loved. His voice had a slow southern drawl that sounded sexy as hell. He was tall and had blond hair with beautiful blue eyes, like his sister, Bird. Rory wondered what kind of parent would name their child Bird.

She didn't realize she was staring at Jonah until he asked her why she was staring at him. "Why would your parents name your sister Bird?"

Jonah laughed, "Her name is Burdine. She doesn't like that name, so she has always been called Bird. Anything else you want to know?"

"Why do you think I'm always getting into trouble? Bird gets into all kinds of trouble."

"Yes, she does, but she doesn't get thrown in jail. If you don't stop fighting, the judge will send you back to Scotland.

Kane wants to live here and work with us, but if you have to go home, then he'll go with you."

"I do want to go home. There is no place to walk here. Everything is cement and buildings. When you walk, men harass you. Don't you miss having green hills around you? Bird told me you guys grew up where it was green and water all around with alligators. I would be scared the alligators would get my wee children. I wouldn't want to let them outside."

It was Jonah's turn to chuckle. He liked her Scottish accent and the different words she used when she communicated. "It's not that bad. We try to keep the gators away from homes." He looked over at her, "So you think about having wee ones, do you?"

"Doesn't everyone think about the children they'll have?"

"I don't know."

"You should think about it. How old are you?"

"I'm thirty-six. And what does my age have to do with anything?"

"Well, you want to have babies before you're too old to play with them."

"I have plenty of years before I have to worry about old age." He pulled up to Missy's house, where Rory stayed until escrow closed on Kane's house. "Stay out of trouble."

"I will," Rory smirked as she got out of the vehicle and walked away.

Most of the time, Jonah stayed out of his Band of Navy Seals family's lives, but he sometimes helped their family since he's the lawyer for them. So far, Rory has been the only one in the band's family he's gone to court with. When Kane Walsh brought his sister from Scotland back to the United States, it almost knocked him over how beautiful she was. He kept telling himself she was Kane's sister, and he had to stop thinking how sexy her body looked in those tight jeans.

He called Kane and told him the Judge let Rory off. "Can you please tell her to stop going to clubs alone? Dude, she's going to get attacked, or anything can happen to her."

Kane laughed out loud. He couldn't picture his sister getting attacked by anyone who would be stupid enough to try attacking her. "Stop worrying about Rory. She can take care of herself. I'll tell her to stay out of fights. Scotland is different. Everyone knows each other, and everyone is happy to see you when you go to the pub. Here the women are always trying to outdo each other, and she's not used to that. Everyone loved her in Scotland. Rory was a favorite because she sang so sweet."

Jonah could believe that. "Why is she a behavioral therapist? That is one of the worst jobs someone as beautiful as Rory can have."

"She can take care of herself. We don't have to worry about her. So, she told you she starts work on Monday?"

"Yes, she did. She also said you told her to get a job."

"Well, yes. That will keep her busy, and she'll stay out of trouble. Anything else?"

Jonah paused. He decided not to push the issue. Kane was probably right. "No, that's all."

"Thank you, Jonah. Let me know what I owe you."

"If you can keep your sister out of trouble, that's my payment."

"I'll try. Now that Rory's working, it shouldn't be so hard."

Jonah didn't think that would make all the difference, but he was hopeful. He'd promised Ash to help him, so he headed over to his house. As he pulled onto the driveway, he spotted Ash on top of the three-story Victorian house. "Damn it, Ash. Are you trying to kill yourself?"

Ash laughed, "Take your jacket and tie off and come up here. The ladder is on the other side of the house."

Jonah reluctantly put his jacket and tie in his vehicle and

rolled up the sleeves of his white shirt. Then, he climbed up the damn rickety ladder. "Where the hell did you find this ladder?"

"Under the house."

"It's older than this Victorian house, and this is the one we use. Who makes wooden ladders anymore? What are we going to do up here?"

"The eaves are missing some of those scallops. We had some made for us, but I need help holding them while my carpenter connects them to the eaves."

"Shouldn't we be standing on a ladder under the eaves? It would be easier to make sure it's hammered straight. Are we going to hang over the roof?"

"No, I have someone to do that. Rory, are you ready?"

"Yes, here I am," she said, climbing to the top of the ladder smiling at them.

"We'll hold these up to the eaves while you hammer the nails into the wood."

Jonah couldn't breathe. Why the hell was Rory standing on top of a rickety ladder smiling with a large hammer in her hand? "What the fuck are you doing? You'll fall to your death."

"I'm fixing Ash's eaves."

"Are you crazy? Get off of that damn ladder before you break your damn neck." Jonah reached for her and almost fell.

"I'm going to ignore your tone of voice. Ash asked for my help. Now, stop moving around, or you are going to take me and you both down."

"I just dropped you off at Missy's."

"I know you did. I had to get my vehicle. Calm down Jonah, I'm a carpenter. I know what I'm doing."

"What do you mean you're a carpenter? I thought you

were a damn psychiatric therapist who worked with fucking crazy criminals."

Rory decided to ignore the fact that he was losing his cool as if she was married to him. "I build stuff as well. I make furniture and other things. I have worked on houses since I was thirteen. I used to go with my Grandpa every summer and holiday. I thought you knew this. Who do you think fixed the staircase at the safe house?"

"I just assumed a repairman fixed it," he bit. Jonah looked over at Ash, "Let's get this finished so she can get off that damn ladder." Jonah was impressed watching Rory. She knew what she was doing. He watched as she measured and hammered. Then, in no time at all, they were finished. Jonah held his breath as she climbed down the damn ladder.

"Dinner is ready," Willow said as she walked out the door, followed by Ruby.

"Am I staying for dinner then?" Rory asked as she hugged Ruby.

"Yes, you are, and so are you, Jonah."

"Hey, I won't argue with eating good food. I remember what a good cook you are."

Jonah couldn't take his eyes off of Rory. She seemed different now that he knew she wasn't just a party girl who always got into trouble. He forced himself to stop watching her hoping she wouldn't catch him and think he's some type of weirdo. "Dinner was delicious. Thank you for inviting me," Jonah said, hugging Willow.

"I'm glad you were here to help and share our dinner." Willow threaded her arm with Rory's and walked out the back, and they sat on the porch swing. "Why was Jonah watching you the entire night?"

"I don't know. Maybe he's still angry about going to court with me."

"I think Jonah wants you. I can tell by the way he looks at

you. Jonah loves women, and they love him. I mean, that southern drawl of his right. I've only seen a few women he's been with, and I've known him a long time. He has never watched those women as he watched you. Yep, he wants you," she concluded.

"Wants me," Rory let out in shock horror. "Do you mean Jonah wants to make love to me? I've never made love with a man before. I'm a virgin. I'm saving myself for my husband. I made a promise to my grandfather. I won't break it for anyone. So he can't have me."

Willow threw her arms around her friend and hugged her. "You are amazing. I swear you make me want to cry. Every time I see you, I find out something more spectacular about you. You are so lucky to have had the relationship you had with your grandpa."

Rory blushed before replying, "I know. I loved him so much. Sometimes I can feel him with me. I feel like he can hear me when I speak to him."

"I'm sure he can hear you. Your grandfather must have been so proud of you."

"We argued all the time. Grandfather wanted people to think he was a grumpy old man. But he wasn't. When we argued, it only lasted a couple of minutes. My sister was more interested in working on the farm. Elspeth loves that farm. I wanted to be with grandpa wherever he went, I went. He taught me everything he knew. I miss him so much. I don't have casual sex with anyone. Not even the handsome Jonah Brewer. No matter how tempting he is."

2

Jonah had to get the hell away from Rory. He knew from the beginning he should have left before Willow served dinner. He's made sure he's only been around Rory for a little while each time he was with her. Too long near her made his palms itch to touch her. He decided to take a run when he got to the safe house. He had to get Rory off his mind. He ran five miles before he turned around and headed back to the house. He had just finished his shower when Kane walked in. "Did you know Rory was helping Ash with his roof? The damn ladder he has is older than the Victorian house and made out of wood. The damn thing is so rickety it needs to be put in the burn pile. You have to talk to her."

"What about?"

"Have you heard a word I said?"

"You want me to talk to Rory about how old Ash's ladder is?"

"I want you to tell her to stay the hell off that ladder. She'll fall and break her neck. The house is three stories and she was hanging scallops on the very top of his house."

"Have you ever tried telling Bird anything? Believe me, as much as Bird never listens to you, Rory is five times worse. I stopped trying to tell her what to do when she was three years old. Do you know where Rory is right now?"

"She was at Ash's earlier. I'm not sure she's still there or not. Why have you been hunting her?"

"I want to go furniture shopping tomorrow, and I want to get everything we need in one day."

Jonah laughed until he started coughing. "Have you ever been shopping with a woman?"

"Yes, I bought my bedroom set when I turned sixteen. My old one was way too small for me. My grandfather's friend took me. It took me ten minutes. I walked in, saw what I wanted, and bought it. Ten minutes, in and out."

"Good luck with that. Believe me, women here are a different lot. Everything has to match all the way down to the throw on the bed. I volunteered to take Bird when she was buying furniture for her house. It was a nightmare. We shopped for six hours, and she purchased one room of furniture. After that, I refused to go with her again. Maybe Rory is different. I mean, she's not like most women I know."

"What do you mean?" Kane asked, looking at Jonah with a frown on his face.

"She is a psychiatric therapist. She is a carpenter. She's a farmer. She has numerous belts in martial arts. She is a cook we can only dream about. Is there anything she can't do?"

"Not really. Rory was one of those kids who never stopped. She drove my grandfather crazy, so he put her in everything he could think to put her in. When she was out of school, he took her with him to work. In the beginning, he wanted to keep her busy, but she learned so fast he enjoyed having her with him. They were very close. When our grandfather died, I knew I had to bring Rory here with me. She would have grieved herself to the grave. She's a giver. Rory likes taking care of everyone. Our sister is Rory's identical twin, but she's content to work the farm, and that fills her up, I guess you could call it."

"Hmm, I'm glad I only have one sister who is married and has her husband to take care of her."

Austin came around the corner in his wheelchair. "Jonah, I have an assignment for you."

Jonah was glad he was being sent away on an assignment. "Tell me about it."

"You will be guarding a teenager while she goes to her mother's in Greece. You pick her up tomorrow. Here is her file and everything you need to know. Your plane ticket is also there."

"Thanks, I have friends in Greece. Maybe I'll see them after I drop off the young lady. It should be a breeze."

"Read the report."

"I will." Jonah went to his room and was asleep before he looked at the files. Early the following morning, when his car showed up, he went over all the papers in the file. The girl was seventeen and was a runaway. She decided to go back home because she was tired of living on the streets in Los Angeles.

Jonah didn't understand why she lived on the streets if they could afford to pay for the Band of Navy Seals, who wasn't cheap to take her home. He would find out soon, though. The car pulled up to a bungalow-style house across from the beach. When he knocked on the door, a beautiful redhead opened. Standing behind her was the teen.

"Hi, I'm Jonah Brewer. I'm here to pick up Angela Baros. I'm from the Band of Navy Seals."

"Hello, Mr. Brewer. May I see your I.D?"

Jonah showed his I.D.

"Thank you, my name is Evelyn Wesson, and this is Angela Baros. I'll be going with you to Greece as a chaperone. I was contacted by Angela's mother, who was very worried about her daughter. I hope that's alright with you."

"It's fine with me, but I need to call her mother to make sure this is what she wants. She is, after all, the one paying the bill."

"We'll be getting our bags," Evelyn said, smiling.

Jonah walked over to the car and told the driver they were getting their bags as he made his phone call. "Hello, Mrs. Baros, this is Jonah Brewer, Band of Navy Seals. I'm wanting to verify that Evelyn Wesson will also be going with us to Greece."

"Yes, Evelyn is my friend. She is the one Angela called when she was ready to come back home."

"Great, we'll see you tomorrow."

Jonah walked up and took the bags from Evelyn as she walked out of the house. I talked to Mrs. Baros, so I guess we'll all be flying to Greece. Angela, if you need anything, don't hesitate to ask."

"No, I don't need anything. Thank you."

"Why are you so sad?"

Angela looked at him. They were all three sitting in the back of the limo. "Why do you think I'm sad?"

"You haven't smiled since I've picked you up."

"I ran away from home. I came all the way to the United States hunting for someone, but he's nowhere around."

"What's his name?"

She looked away before speaking, "His name is Jayden Robertson. He's in the Marines. He told me he loved me, but he had to leave. I waited an entire month for him to call me. After that, I knew I would have to find him myself. I didn't think my mother would put a stop to my credit cards. A tear fell down her cheek. Jonah handed her a tissue."

"Why do you need to get in touch with him?"

Another tear fell. Angela looked at Jonah. "Everyone is going to know pretty soon. I'm having a baby."

Both the information and the tone she said it in hit Jonah hard and fast. Jonah got up and sat next to her, and pulled her into his arms. He was happy she didn't recoil. This poor girl felt all alone. She was used by a bastard who probably didn't even give her his real name. Jonah would check him out. He would make sure she didn't feel ashamed for being pregnant.

"How far along are you?"

"A few months. My mother is going to kill me. She'll make me get rid of it," she sobbed.

"I'm sure she won't do that. When will you be eighteen?"

"In four months."

"Wait. Are you saying you're going to have a baby?" Evelyn demanded. She had just drunk another one of those little vodka bottles, it was her fourth one. She grabbed the first one and downed it as if to bring her back to reality the moment the words left Angela's mouth.

"Yes, and this is why I didn't tell you or my mother. Both of you are so afraid of something not looking good. You don't care about my feelings."

"Angie, that isn't true, sweetheart; you can come to me for anything. You know how much your mom loves you. I love you as well, and you know it. Your mother was scared to death when you ran away. She didn't know where you were."

"I asked her if I could talk to her numerous times. She never had time to talk to me. What was I supposed to do? I really thought I would find Jayden. He said he was in San Diego. Why would he lie to me? He told me he loved me."

Jonah hugged her tighter wanting to take the hurt he was sure she was feeling away. "I will make sure everything is good with your mother before I leave."

"You will?"

"Yes. Now, we are at the airport, so dry your eyes. This is a time for celebrating a new life."

"Okay."

"Angie, I'll help you talk to your mother. But you have to know this will change your entire life. You won't be able to run with your friends or take off to spend the night with one of them. You know their parents won't want them around you. Have you thought about all of this?"

"Yes, Evelyn, I have. That's why I ran away. I was so scared. I don't know how to take care of a baby. I've never been around a baby."

Soon they walked on the plane, and Evelyn sat next to Angie. "You're my godchild. I'll help you through this, I promise you. Don't be scared. If you want to live with me, you can. But this is your child. You are going to give birth to a baby. That baby will be yours to take care of. How will you support it?"

"I'll get a job."

"You haven't finished high school. How will you get a job? Who will watch the baby while you are at work?"

"I don't know yet. I'm sorry I'm causing all this trouble. I don't know what to do."

"We'll figure it all out when we are with your mother," Evelyn said as she kissed her forehead.

Angie nodded her head and wiped her eyes. She slept for most of the ride home. Evelyn looked at Jonah and smiled. "Why is your company called Band of Navy Seals?"

"Because we are all ex-Navy Seals. So, Angie is your goddaughter. Will you take care of her if her mom tries to make her get rid of the baby?"

"Mary would never make Angie do that. It's against her religion. Besides, Angie is all she has left in her family. Her husband and two boys died in a plane crash six years ago."

"That must have been hard on them."

"Yes. It was very hard. All Mary's kids were my godchildren."

"Are you related?"

"No, we grew up together. I grew up in Greece. I go back to Greece once or twice a year. My home is in Los Angeles now. I love the nightlife and the people. There isn't anything I don't like about it."

"So all the cement and high-rise buildings don't bother you."

"Are you kidding? I love it. That's what I like the most. Hang on," she dipped into her purse and passed it to him, "here's my card. Call me when I get home, and we'll hit the clubs together."

"Sure." He put the card in his pocket before asking, "What do you do for a living?"

"I'm a model. Been modeling since I was fifteen. I left home and moved to California."

"So you thought that maybe Angie thought if you did it, she could too. Didn't imagine her chasing the father of her child, did you?"

"That's exactly what I thought. Who would have thought? I thought she told her mom everything. So are you going to give me a call?"

"I'd have to be crazy not to. Here's my card. Let me know when you get home."

Evelyn couldn't take her eyes off the handsome Jonah Brewer. She would let him take her tonight if he wanted. She would have to find a way to let him know. "Are you single, Jonah?"

"I wouldn't have taken your card if I wasn't single. What about you? Do you have someone in your life?"

"No, I don't. I never just date one man. I enjoy men too much for that. But, I might change for you. Maybe we could get together after Angie is reunited with Mary."

"I already made plans with some friends. But I'll definitely be calling you when we get home."

"I'm looking forward to having you for an entire night all to myself."

Jonah smiled until Rory's face popped in his head. He shook his head until her image was gone. *That is never going to happen. She's Kane's sister. But then again, Bird is my sister, and my buddy married her. Oh, hell no. I'm never going to marry Rory Walsh. What the hell is the matter with me? I've never even kissed the woman, and I'm not going to either.*

3

"Is Jonah still in Greece?" Rory asked Bird, Jonah's sister.

"Yes, he might be back by now. He was there when I talked to him. He decided to make it a vacation. He has some friends there, plus he told me he met a woman who has taken a liking to him. I swear that brother of mine has had women after him since he was thirteen."

Willow looked at Bird to tell her with her eyes to shut up. She thought that Rory might like Jonah a little more than just as a friend. She saw the hurt look in her eyes only because she was looking. It lasted a split second. But she saw it. It made her sad because Jonah, she knew, didn't date virgins.

Rory kept on putting the baby's bed together, not letting on that she wished Jonah would look at her like he wanted to hook up with her. "You'll have to get a bigger house if you keep having babies, Bird."

"I was going to talk to you about that, Rory. I absolutely love the pretty way you painted this crib. You're very talented. Thank you for this gift. I have a project I want to hire you for. I saw how you did Brinley's nursery, and I would love for you to do the new baby's room. Also, Gracie would like you to paint a mural in her room. I know you are working at that prison behavioral center, but you can do it whenever you want. I'm not going to put a time schedule on it or anything. But I've never seen such a beautiful mural. I can have everything delivered to wherever you want to work. I'm not pressuring you or anything. What do you think?"

"I would love to paint a mural in the children's rooms. How about when I get finished here, you tell me what you like, and I'll draw up some designs for you."

"Yes, thank you! I am going to have some work done in my house and knock a wall down, so we have one big room. That way, the children will be able to see me, and I can see them when I'm making dinner."

"I thought Killian did the cooking," Willow said with a big smile on her face.

"He does the grilling. I do the cooking. We don't grill every night. Sometimes Killian's gone for a week at a time."

Rory and Willow both smiled. They knew Bird always wanted Killian home with her and the babies. "You should add a section to your family room," Rory said, looking around the room.

"Wow, what a great idea. I'll talk to the contractor and see what he says.

"I would. You have all this space outside. I used to help my granddad. He would rebuild homes for people."

"You're a charm," she said, hugging Rory. "By the way, do you like Temecula?"

"Yes, it's beautiful out here. You have the sea close by, and these vineyards are beautiful. I hate living in the city. I can't breathe in that place. The place I work in is even worse. There are homeless people everywhere. They sleep on the sidewalk in front of doorways. I visit with them as much as I can. All they want is someone to talk to them for a while. There is a boy about eighteen. I see him carrying his guitar around. The others say he's a good kid. He doesn't do drugs. He lost his job and can't afford to rent a place. I'll try talking to him the next time I see him."

"What the hell are you talking about? Damn it, Rory, I told you that place was too dangerous for you," Jonah said, walking into the room. He bent and gave Bird a kiss as he reached her.

Rory didn't look at him, "It's my job. I have to be going. Bird, if you will email me and let me know what you would like for the bedrooms, I'll draw a few pictures up for you to look at. Send me some pictures if you find anything if you see anything in a magazine or somewhere else."

"Okay, I guess I'll see you two around," Willow said, hopping up. She thought Rory must have forgotten they came together.

"Thank you guys for helping me. Rory, I'll email you soon."

Rory nodded her head and walked outside.

Jonah stared after Rory. "Why the hell did she leave so fast?"

"Why did you yell at her? Damn it, Jonah, Rory is going to paint murals in some of the children's rooms. Leave her alone. She's my friend."

"I'm concerned for her safety. She works in the roughest area in the city. I didn't mean to upset her."

"Why are you so concerned? Rory can take care of herself. She makes friends with everyone she meets." Before Jonah could say anything about the scuffles Rory's gotten herself into, Bird hurried and added, "Except with mean people. She doesn't make friends with mean people. Actually, why are you here? I thought you would be staying in Greece longer since you met a woman there."

"She lives in Los Angeles. We are going out for dinner tonight."

"Don't forget Willow's bar-b-que next Saturday."

"I have it on my phone. Now, are you going to offer me anything to drink? Have you seen Piper lately? I want to know if she can landscape the back of my property. I have five acres behind my house that I want to be turned into a calm oasis. The pond has that underground natural spring that I want to make better use of."

"That would be beautiful. I talked to Piper yesterday. She's home. You should call her before she becomes too busy. She is always off doing something. Let's call her now."

Before he could say anything, Bird had made the phone call. She said hi to Piper then handed Jonah the phone. He explained what he wanted, and Piper said she would meet him at his place in the morning at seven. He handed the phone back to his sister. "She'll meet me at seven in the morning."

"Will you be home by then?"

"I'll make sure I am. I'll talk to you later. I had a call from Granny. She's coming for a visit next week. She said she'll stay with you because she has to help with the little ones."

Bird jumped up. "Oh, I almost forgot. I have so much to do before Granny gets here. I can't wait to see her."

"She's bringing a few of her friends with her. They are only staying a few days, though, while Granny is staying longer."

"What? Who is she bringing?"

"Her voodoo ladies. She wants to clean your house."

"They did that when I bought the house. Let her clean your home instead. My house is free of all spirits."

Jonah laughed as he walked out the door. Then, he turned around, "I told her the spirits were afraid to come to my house."

4

Rory arrived at work early Monday morning like she always did. She liked to bring coffee and donuts to the group of homeless people who she visited. They were waiting for her. She passed the cups and donuts around, and they talked about everything until it was time she went inside. Rory would rather stay out and visit with the homeless people. Those inside were hard to talk to. They were all horrid hateful killers who she hated to be around. She wished she hadn't taken on this job. It gave her a big headache.

"You be careful inside that building," one of the homeless ladies told her. "Those in there are crazy. You watch yourself. I've heard horrible stories about these people."

Rory nodded and took out her clearance card as she stepped inside the hell hole where she worked.

Jonah watched from down the street. He shook his head, knowing Rory wouldn't listen to a word he said. He would come back when it was time she got off work.

Rory walked into the room where she talked to each person. They liked her less than she liked them. They constantly threatened to do things to her. Rory ignored them most of the time. "Hello, Mike."

"My name is Mikey!" he screamed in her face.

"You're in your forties, and you still want to be called Mikey?"

"Fuck you! Yes, I do! My mother called me Mikey, so that is my name!"

"You killed your mother and your sister and her two children. I'm sure she wouldn't call you Mikey if she was here right now," Rory said.

The man flew across the table. Rory had him down and under her boot before he knew what to do. "Don't you ever come after me," she whispered so the camera couldn't hear her. "I will kill you without blinking. Did you get that?" she said, pushing her boot harder between his shoulder blades.

"Help, help! The bitch is trying to kill me!" Mike shouted for help.

"What's the matter, Mikey? You can't beat this woman like the other ones you killed." Jackson looked over at Rory while he pushed Mike out of the room. He was back in one minute, as Rory knew he would be. "Damn it, Rory. Don't piss them off. They'll kill you."

"I'm trying to get him to see what he's done. If I have to piss him off, I will. This is my job. It's what I get paid for. I don't baby talk any of them."

Jackson shook his head. "There is some chatter going around that the prisoners are going to try something. So you should stay home for a couple of weeks. I don't want to scare you, but they will hurt you really bad before killing you. You know that don't you?"

"What do you mean? If you've heard something, then put extra security in. Keep them in lock-up."

"We are putting together something now."

"What's to put together. Keep all of them in lock-up.

They'll kill all of you. These guys are all crazy. I've talked to every one of them. I don't mean crazy in the head like most crazy people. These men are the worst kind of crazy. They won't just kill you. First, they'll cut small parts off, and then they'll cut some more pieces off until they get bored and move on to the next guard."

"Why don't you leave early? Mike will tell the others how good you can fight, then they'll all want to fight you."

"I'll leave early, but I'll be back tomorrow. You have wee ones. You should worry about yourself. Go home. Find a different place to work. So your children will still have a father."

Rory walked out of the building and out of the locked gate. She heard someone playing the guitar and looked around. The young man was playing music for his homeless friends so she walked over and listened to him. His voice was outstanding. He sang three more songs before he stopped. "You have a beautiful voice. Do you know any songs from Scotland?"

He started playing a song Rory recognized. She started singing and all she could think of was home. Rory missed home. When the song ended, she wiped a tear from her cheek.

"Why do you stay here if you miss home so much?"

"My brother is here. I don't want to leave him without family."

"You're a good sister and a great singer. My name is Alex Fox," he said, holding his hand out."

"Hi, Alex, my name is Rory Walsh. There's a rumor something might be happening with men in there," she said, motioning to the prison behind her. It was called a prison, but it only held forty of the country's most dangerous and craziest men. "You might want to find a different place to stay. Until this unease is over."

"Thank you for telling me." He turned to the group. Did you hear that? "Let's move our belongings."

Before Rory knew what was happening, the homeless people were packing up their camp. She looked at Alex, "I have a bar-b-que this weekend. There will be some people there I want you to meet. Do you want me to pick you up?"

"Sure, I would love that."

"Where will you be? Oh, hang on. Here is my card. Call me Saturday morning, and I'll pick you up," she looked at the homeless people. "Where should I bring the coffee and donuts?"

They gave her an address and Rory left, not knowing about the man watching her down the street. Jonah shook his head. *Does she not have friends? She has to make friends with the homeless people.* He watched her walk to her car and waited until she drove away.

He followed her through the city. She stopped and bought flowers from a lady on the side of the street. Jonah watched as she hugged the woman and bought another bunch of flowers. He smiled to himself. Then she stopped and ran across the street to purchase some sliced fruit sprinkled with chili powder. He didn't know what she was doing when he saw her stop at the cemetery and she put flowers on a gravesite. He waited until she left, then he got out and walked over to see who she knew at the cemetery. The marker said the unknown woman died two months ago. He wondered if she was one of the homeless people. As he was leaving, another woman walked up and looked at the flowers.

"Do you know what her name was?" he asked the woman.

"Yeah, it was Helen. She was my sister. She got hooked on drugs and overdosed. She was twenty-three."

"Sorry for your loss. What was her last name?"

"Flynn. Her name was Helen Flynn, only twenty-three

years old when she died. She left behind four kids. I'm raising them."

Jonah thought the woman looked to be about thirty. "Again, I'm sorry for your loss and theirs."

The woman shook her head. "We are so much better off without her. I know that sounds terrible. We don't have to listen to her screaming for drugs. Or taking all the money the children got from the State. The lady that just left brings flowers once a week. I asked her once why she brought flowers. Do you know what she told me?"

"No."

"She told me that she named the dead woman Tammy because the dead have to have a name. So Jesus knows where to find her. So I thought to myself, *why would Jesus come and get Helen*? But Helen wasn't always a drug addict, and I was ashamed of myself for thinking she wasn't good enough. Because she was. She really was. I work in the office here. I hate to admit I didn't claim my sister. I would never have been able to pay for her burial. I have a hard time taking care of her children. My fiancé left me when I took them in."

"He sounds like a jerk to me."

"Yeah, that's what I thought as well."

Jonah walked away. He took out his phone and bought Helen Flynn a headstone. He drove away thinking Rory Walsh was full of surprises.

~

SATURDAY, Jonah drove to Evelyn's. He wished he hadn't invited her to the bar-b-que. She was fun for a while, but she had three thoughts in her head, and that was partying, booze, and sex. Jonah didn't mind the sex, but he would like for her to be sober once in a while. He preferred his women to not be full of alcohol when they had sex. That's why after only a few dates, he was wanting to break it off with her.

"Jonah, do you think I should bring some booze? I like vodka. A lot of times they only have beer at bar-b-ques."

"No, I'm sure there will be plenty of booze to go around. My friends don't drink much alcohol. They have children. But they love ice tea."

She shuddered like he'd said something unimaginable. "They have children on purpose? Why do women want to bring kids into the world? This is not a good place for kids anymore, too many drugs and killings. I never want children."

"Yes, I know." Jonah chuckled, remembering Rory said she wanted lots of wee ones.

"Why are you laughing?"

"I'm sorry, I was thinking of something else. Are you ready?"

"Yes. Let me grab my sweater."

The driveway was packed, so Jonah parked on the road. It looked like everyone they knew was here. He heard laughing as he walked to the backyard where his friends were. He looked around and didn't see Rory anywhere. Willow and Ash greeted them, and Jonah introduced Evelyn to everyone.

"Grab you something to drink," Ash said, turning the steak.

"I'll have a martini if you don't mind. If you don't have that, I'll have vodka on ice."

"I'll get her something," Jonah said, walking over to the outside fridge. "Since it's only three, how about some ice tea?"

"When I'm an old lady, I'll drink tea. I want something with vodka in it."

Jonah poured some vodka in a glass with mostly grapefruit juice. He handed it to Evelyn, "Here you go."

"Thank you," she took a drink, "yummy. This is what I needed. Let's go mingle. As they walked across the deck, Rory showed up with the homeless guy. Jonah couldn't believe she brought a homeless person to Willow's house. They headed for Polly.

"Polly, this is Alex. I told you about him."

"Hello, Alex. I'm so happy to meet you. Rory has been singing your praises."

Alex smiled, he knew he was staring, but he couldn't help it. He was talking to Sugar, who was on the top of the country charts. He saw Taylor laughing with a beautiful girl. They were both famous singers. Then Bird Suneagle walked up and hugged Rory; she was a renowned singer-songwriter.

"Willow, you've been working hard, I see. This is beautiful."

"Don't you love these lights? Wait until the sun goes down. It is so pretty. Thank you so much for helping me choose the deck arbors. They go perfectly with this Victorian home. Is this your friend?"

"Yes, Alex, this is Willow Beckham. She lives here with her husband, Ash." Rory smiled because Alex looked like he just saw his all-time idols. And she guessed he did by the way he was staring at Polly.

"Hi Willow, thank you for letting me come to your house. A lot of people wouldn't want a homeless person in their homes."

"Hey, we all go through rough times. That makes us stronger, don't you think?"

"Yes, I do, thank you."

"I can't wait to hear you sing. Would you sing us a song now?" Polly asked, handing him a guitar.

"Sure, is there any particular song you want to hear?"

"Have you written one that you like?"

Alex nodded and sat on the barstool. He plucked the

strings and started singing. Alex sang three songs, then he started playing the song Rory sang that day. She smiled and started singing along.

Jonah drifted over and listened to them. Rory sang another song with Alex, was there anything she couldn't do? Jonah admitted Alex was a good singer. Taylor and Missy came over, and Taylor sang a song. Jonah smiled at the group. He saw Kane walk up, and he put his arm around his sister. She took the guitar and sang a song with Kane as she played. He looked around for Evelyn and saw she was at the fridge pouring herself another drink. *Damn.*

RORY SAW JONAH and his girlfriend sitting on the sofa. The woman was kissing him like they were alone in a bedroom. She saw Jonah take the woman's arms from around his neck. He looked embarrassed, and he should be. She heard Polly talking to Alex and she agreed to listen to some of his songs.

"Alex, how would you like to record that first song you sang?"

"Are you kidding me? My God, that would be wonderful! That's what I've always wanted. I would love to record my song. Then, I could finally call my parents and let them know I'm okay." His smile was so big it covered his face. He ran both hands through his hair, not believing what he was being offered. He knew his eyes were starting to glisten from holding tears in.

"How about if you came to our house on Wednesday."

"You want me to come to your house?" She nodded, adding a welcoming smile. "Yes, I would love to do that. Thank you."

"I will get my manager on the phone and he can help you out when you go to Nashville."

"Thank you," he turned and looked at Rory. "Thank you for everything."

"You're welcome. I think dinner is ready."

Missy looked over at Alex, "Hi Alex, I'm Missy Wesson. I'm off to Nashville on Friday. Instead of taking a bus, I have an extra ticket you can use. I'll help you get all set up while I'm there."

"Really, that would be so awesome. Are you sure? You don't even know me."

"Of course, I'm sure. I enjoy helping people out if I can. I've had people help me out before. I have a studio apartment in Nashville you can stay in while you get started."

"What? No, I can find a place. But thank you."

"I'll pick you up on Friday," Missy said, ignoring what he said.

Rory smiled at her friend. Missy did what she wanted to do, and that was helping people. Missy had a way of helping everyone. Alex would find out on Friday how stubborn Missy could be.

"Thank you for inviting me to your bar-b-que. I had the best time."

Willow put her arm through Rory's. "I wish you could stay a little longer."

"I have to take Alex downtown. And I've been up since three this morning, and it's hitting me now."

"I'll take Alex. He can stay longer. Polly wants to hear him sing more songs," Zane said, walking to where Rory stood talking with Willow.

"Thank you, Zane. Alex, Zane will be taking you back to where you're staying, so you can stay longer if you want."

"Sure, thank you—thanks Rory, for everything you've done for me."

"You're so welcome. When you become famous, I'll come to your concert. I can tell people I knew Alex Fox before he became famous," she smiled at him. "It takes a lot of hard work. But if you love what you do, then it'll be worth it."

"Do you love what you do?"

"No, I love painting and I enjoyed helping my grandfather. I don't love or even like working at that hell hole where I work. I'm going to give notice. Thank you for helping me see something I always tell other people to do."

He laughed and hugged her. "Bye, Rory. I'm sure I'll be seeing you around. Thanks for letting me shower before we came here."

"Bye, Alex. Let me give you some advice. Whatever Missy Wesson suggests you do, then do it. She knows what she's talking about. On everything. She's one of those people that has the golden touch."

"Thanks. I'll listen to Missy then."

5

Jonah felt like he was a damn stalker. He promised this would be the last day he would follow Rory. She made her stop at the homeless camp with her coffees and donuts. He followed her to her job, then he went to the safe house. Kane was there when he walked in.

"How did your girlfriend feel Sunday morning?"

"I don't know. I haven't seen Evelyn since I dropped her off."

"You've got to be kidding. The woman was all over you before you left."

"Sometimes, you don't want a woman to be all over you. I think it's time I stopped going out with Evelyn. I would have told her Saturday night if she had been sober. She has a drinking problem, and I don't need the stress right now. Did you know your sister has breakfast with homeless people? You need to watch out for her. That place where she works is too damn dangerous. I checked it out. Those men are crazy dangerous. They are cut-throats. They are the worst killers in our country. I know you say Rory can take care of herself, but if anything happens there, and those men get loose, they won't only kill her, they'll rape her. Every one of those fuckers will take turns. You need to get her to quit. She's been doing side jobs, painting murals, so that should keep her busy. Do something before it's too late."

Kane saw how serious Jonah was. It shook him up. He decided he would talk to Rory that night and told Jonah he would.

Jonah couldn't believe this guy, "Tonight? Call her and tell her to leave now."

"You are the one who wanted me to tell her to get a job."

"What? Don't blame me. And even if I did, why did she have to apply at the most dangerous place in the country?"

Before Kane could continue what was about to become an argument or at least a blaming game, Austin came over and interrupted them, "Hello, Jonah, Kane. You two are just the ones I wanted to see. I'm sending you to a little town in Idaho. There is a family there who needs you. Here's the file. You'll have to leave right away."

"Who's going to watch over Rory while she's working at that damn place?" Jonah demanded to know.

"Does Rory need someone to watch over her?" Austin asked, frowning.

Kane shrugged, "Jonah thinks she needs to quit her job. I was going to talk to her about it tonight."

"I'll talk to her. I'll call her and tell her to bring her things here, she can stay the night. Don't worry about Rory. I'll talk her into quitting her job."

Jonah shook his head. Austin thought it would be so easy. "How the hell will you talk her into staying the night?"

"I'll tell her no one is here, and I've been feeling strange. She has such a caring heart she won't even question me."

Jonah and Kane laughed; Jonah couldn't believe Austin knew more about Rory than he did. She has never shown him the caring side of her personality. He knew she was friendly and maybe, even adorable. Perhaps he was thinking more about her than he should. Sometimes she made you want to pull her into your arms and kiss her until she kissed you back. *Stop right there Jonah, you do not date your friend's sister. What about Killian? He dated my sister and married her.*

"Your flight leaves in two hours, so you better get moving," Austin interrupted his thoughts.

"When are you calling Rory?" Jonah asked before he went up to get his bag.

"I'll go in and call her right now."

"Tell her she needs to quit that job. That she's getting so busy with her painting jobs, she'll have to hire help. Say what you have to just to get her away from that damn job."

"Wow, you really are serious."

"Just do what you can to keep her away from that place. I have a feeling, and I can't shake it."

"Okay, I'll do what I can."

Not long after they left, Austin called Rory, and she agreed to come and stay the night.

"I'll stop and get pizza; then, we won't have to cook dinner," she told him.

"I'll see you later, sweetie," Austin said as he hung up. He looked up at the sound of footsteps. Jonah stood in the doorway. "She's staying here. I'll talk to her when she gets here. Now, leave before you miss your plane."

"Why do you have this feeling?" Kane asked as they walked out the door.

"I don't know. I pray it's just a stupid feeling. We know I've had those before. I guess I have too much of my granny in me."

"We also know you've had feelings that do lead to something. More often than the other way." Kane took out his phone and punched in some numbers. A voice answered on the other end. "Hello, Rory, I'm going to be out of town for a while. I can't worry about you the entire time I'm gone. I want this to be your last day of work." He looked at his phone then put it back in his pocket.

"What did she say?"

"She hung up on me."

Jonah smirked, "I thought that went too smooth."

"Oh yeah, Rory will do the right thing. That's how she is. Since she was a wee little girl, she tried to make everything right for our family. I think she wanted our grandfather to be proud of her. So he didn't think we were a burden. We moved in with our grandpa after our parents and grandma died in an accident. Rory made life easy for us growing up. She went to the Pub with grandpa and me. Rory can drink whiskey and stay up longer than most of us. She's a good friend and sister. Elspeth, our sister, worked the farm, and she liked hanging out with her friends who lived nearby. Everyone who knows Rory loves her."

"I'm close with my sister, Bird, as well. I'm happy Killian has to watch over Bird now. She can keep you on your toes."

"I have come to realize that, watching her." Kane replied with a slight chuckle. "I'll call Rory when she gets off work. I'm sure she'll want to give them notice. But, in all fairness, I've always thought of Rory as someone who could take care of herself. We had this man Jim who lived on the farm. He knew everything about martial arts. My grandfather paid him to teach us what he knew. It's come in handy more than I ever thought it would have. When I joined the Seals, I had to use it multiple times. I'm sure you realize by now that she can handle herself."

Jonah wanted to take comfort in that but he knew how

dangerous these men were and he couldn't shake the feeling he was having.

~

"AUSTIN, TELL ME HOW YOU FEEL?"

Austin didn't want to lie to Rory, so he told her the truth. "My legs are tingling. I don't know what is causing it. But it started two days ago. I haven't told anyone about it because I don't want them to get excited if nothing comes of it. I can't stand for them to look at me with pity in their eyes."

"I'm sure what they have in their eyes is more, that they're pissed off over what happened and weren't there to help when you needed them. They are mad at themselves. Tell me how it started."

"The tingling is mostly in my feet, but it goes up my left leg often."

"Have you called Frankie?"

"No, I don't want anyone to know, except you."

"Why just me? I'm no doctor. The doctor told you that you would be able to walk again. Didn't he?"

"Yes, but I'm afraid to get my hopes up."

"I understand that. Sometimes I get my hopes up then it hurts too badly when it doesn't work out the way I thought it would. But you now know that you have feelings in your legs. That means you will walk again. I think you should call Frankie and tell her what's going on."

"She'll want me going for tests and everyone is gone. I'll wait until the guys get back."

"I'll take time off while I'm here. Hell, I can help you as well as any man could."

"Are you sure? Will you get in trouble at work?"

"I gave them a two weeks' notice today. Jonah is so frigging crazy over me working there I just decided to quit. I never did like working there, to be honest. Does that make me a quitter?"

"Fuck no, it doesn't. Aren't you busy painting murals anyway? I'm sure you make good money from that business. If you ever need help, let me know. I used to do some painting when I was in college before I left for the service."

"Did you paint murals?"

"Yes, I would paint murals on store walls. I did some custom work for businesses. My father made custom furniture, and sometimes I would paint the chairs and tables."

"Oh wow. My grandfather did that as well. I helped him often. I did some work for his customers when I wasn't busy with my job. Kane wanted me to come to America with him, plus I didn't want him to be alone again. My twin sister has the farm now, but I can go back anytime if I don't like living here. I promised Kane I would stay a couple of years and give it a chance. I don't want to leave him by himself. He's a good brother, and besides, he worries about me. I don't want him to worry."

"Do you think you'll stay?"

"I'm not sure. I like all of my new friends. So, I'll see." Austin made a face like he was in pain so she asked, "Are you in pain?"

"It started the same time the tingling started."

"Why don't we go swimming? Water is good for you. It works all of your muscles. First we'll go swimming then we'll eat pizza. Go put your swimming trunks on? I'll get mine on. It'll be fun."

"That's a good idea. Okay, I'll take my phone with me in case someone calls."

Rory was ready and getting worried Austin was taking so long. She hoped he didn't fall. That's when she heard him singing a country song.

"I love that song. I didn't know you could sing," she called out.

"I wouldn't call it singing. I just open my mouth and what comes out comes out."

"Do you miss Texas?"

"I have a home there. It's a two thousand acre cattle ranch. I haven't been home since I was injured. I've never told my family about my injury."

"Really? So who's watching your cattle ranch?"

"I have a couple who lives there and a few other workers." He was now behind Rory, "Forget about me, and look at you. Damn, you look good in a swimsuit. How come you are still single?"

"I've just never fallen in love, I suppose. How about you?"

"I had a fiancée once. We were high school sweethearts. I asked her to marry me when we graduated high school. She said yes. When I came back from overseas, she had married a friend of mine."

"What a horrible person. Did she break your heart, or did you find yourself surprised because your heart wasn't as broken as it should have been?"

"Now I know why you're a therapist. You're damn good."

Rory laughed, "I bet she regrets marrying the other guy. I mean, look at how handsome and sexy you are. Who wouldn't want you for a husband?"

"Would you like to marry me?"

"If I wasn't already in love with someone, I would."

"So you're in love."

"Don't breathe a word of what I said. If Kane heard me say that, he wouldn't leave me alone until I spilled the beans."

"My lips are locked." They were now ready for their swim and Austin pushed himself off into the pool. He watched as Rory dove off the diving board. *Jonah is one lucky guy. If only he would open his eyes.*

They swam for an hour before getting out. Rory watched as Austin pulled himself out of the water. He was all muscle. He had no problem lifting his body out of the pool with his arms. "I'll get changed and heat the pizza," she told him, drying herself off with the towel.

"I'm right behind you."

Rory cooked most of the meals when she was home in Scotland. She whipped up some salad to go with the pizza. Dinner was fun. Rory learned more about Austin, and unbeknown to Rory, Austin learned a lot about her.

"So, have you seen your ex-fiancée since you found out she was married?"

"Once. I was shopping with my dad, and she was in the grocery store. I realized how lucky I was that she married someone else. I said hello, and that was it. She's divorced now, with three kids, and she works at the grocery store. She called me once, not long after I got home on leave, long before the divorce. She wanted to meet me somewhere. I told her she should be calling her husband and hung up."

"You were lucky she married him, or you would have married the wrong woman."

"That's what my dad said. I knew when I saw her in the grocery store how close I came to making a mistake. I didn't feel anything except relief. What about you? Have you had a guy you were serious about?"

"No. Not ever."

"You're still waiting."

"I'm waiting to see if something happens."

Austin smiled. Rory was getting sweeter with every conversation. He didn't know why Jonah thought she always got into trouble. He could fall for her if he didn't know how she felt about Jonah. He realized then how exhausted he was. "I guess I'm going to hit the hay," he told her

"What hay?"

"That's a saying. When I say, 'I'm going to hit the hay,' that means I'm going to bed. I guess when people slept on hay back in the day, that's what they said and it stuck."

Rory laughed all the way to her room. Rory was sleeping when something woke her up. She sat up. Rory climbed out of bed and walked down the hall. She pushed Austin's door open. He was lying on the floor holding his leg. Rory rushed into the room. "Austin, are you alright?"

"No, my legs are killing me. Call Frankie. My phone is next to the bed."

As Rory moved more into the room, she realized Austin didn't have a stitch of clothing on. She shut her eyes and tried finding her way to the bed with her eyes closed. She almost stepped on Austin.

"Why the hell are your eyes closed?"

"You're naked."

"You act as if you've never seen a naked man." Austin shook his head, "Never mind." He instinctively knew. *She has never seen a naked man*. He reached over and pulled the top cover off the bed. "There you go. I'm covered up."

"Frankie, this is Rory," she said into the phone.

"Hello, Rory, what has happened? I know you wouldn't call me at two in the morning unless it's something."

"I'm at the safe house with Austin. He's having bad pains in his legs. He started getting a tingling feeling in his feet and legs a couple of days ago."

"He should have called me two days ago!" she blurted out as she sprung out of bed.

"I know he should have called you."

"Rory, I'm right here. Stop talking about me as if I'm not. Give me the phone."

Austin tried sitting up. "Frankie, what should I do?"

"I'm coming over there. Give the phone back to Rory."

"Hello."

"Rory, can you fill the tub with hot water. I'll be there in a bit."

"Okay, drive careful." Rory looked at Austin, "Where are your shorts? You have to get in the tub, and since I've not seen a naked man before, you are wearing your shorts."

Austin laughed. "You go start the water. I'll put swim trunks on."

Rory walked into the bathroom and started filling the tub. "I have something that will make it even better. I'll be right back."

Austin had lowered himself into the water when Rory came back. She poured her bath salts into the water with him.

"Damn it, Rory, now I'm going to smell like a woman."

"No, you won't she lied. Now you will relax. Lay back and close your eyes. Let the lavender scent and the medicinal salts relax you."

"It's hard to relax with you standing there with those tiny shorts on. Is that even considered a top?"

"I'll be right back." Rory ran to her room and got dressed. Then she went back into Austin's bathroom. He was lying back with his eyes closed. Rory smiled. He would smell like a girl. Then she giggled.

"I know I will smell all sweet and flowery, but I don't give a damn. This is so relaxing. I swear I'm buying a gallon of this stuff."

Rory ran in and got him a pillow and put it behind his head. When Frankie got there, Austin was sleeping in the tub. He had bubbles all around him, and the smell was heavenly. She looked at Rory. "Does he know he'll smell like a woman?"

"Yes, I do, and I don't care." He opened his eyes. "What do you think is going on with my legs?"

"You were told you would walk again. I think that time

has come. We are going to take you to the hospital and run some tests on you. The specialist will be waiting for us."

"I have to take my phone. No one else is here to handle things." He looked over at Frankie, "Do we all drive you crazy? Who did we call before Storm married you?"

"I don't mind. All of you are like family to me."

6

Jonah walked into the police building and saw the family waiting. "Hello, are you Greg Simpson?"

"Yes, this is my wife, Dana, and our daughters, Martha and Melissa. We are so happy to meet you guys. Do you think two men will be enough?"

"Yes, why don't we sit down and talk." Kane led them to a room where he saw some chairs. "Tell us what's been going on."

"I hired this guy Fred Travers. He was doing great until my daughter Martha came with me to work one day. At first, he would just ask about my family. Martha told me he was waiting for her after school one day, and he followed her home. It scared her enough. She called me when she got home. I asked him about it. He said he heard something on the news where someone tried grabbing a girl from the same school. I was wary of the way he started acting. Martha is fourteen, and Melissa is eleven. After that day, he started showing up daily at Martha's school. We had reported him to the police. He was no longer working for me because I fired him." His head was now bowed as he fought back the tears thinking of the horrible things this man could have done to his daughter.

"My dad got into a fight with him at my school. Because my dad picked me up and that man was there. When Dad told him to stay away from me, he hit him. Dad beat him up, and the police came. They took him to jail, but he didn't stay there. That night he knocked on my bedroom window. He wanted me to let him in. I screamed, and my dad went outside, and the man stabbed him. My mom hit the man with a bat," Martha interjected in a solemn tone.

Dana, the mom, took over the telling. "The man is crazy. He wants Martha and he is scaring the hell out of us. He follows us everywhere we go. Martha and Melisa aren't even going to school. They are doing their school online. The police haven't been able to find him. But we see him. We went to a hotel and he flattened all of our tires. We know it was him, but we didn't have proof."

"I can only imagine how bad this has been for all of you, but we are here now. He won't get anywhere near any of you. We'll stay at your house with you. If we take you to a safe house, we'd be there forever. What we want to do is catch this guy and make sure he never does this again."

"What if he breaks into my room?" Martha asked.

"You won't be in there. Either Jonah or I will be in there. You four will all be in the same room with the door opened until we catch this guy." Kane looked around, "Things are going to change for your family until we lock this guy up. Do you think you can all do us a favor? How about we follow you home in our own vehicle to see if we can spot him following you."

They followed behind them to see if they could see another car following. Jonah was on his computer as Kane drove. "These are the kind of dangerous people who never give up. He saw Martha once and started acting like a stalker. He stabbed her father. The guy is earnest. He wants this girl and he'll do anything to get her. Maybe he'll show up tonight." He was more summarizing everything for himself than for Kane's benefit.

Kane nodded before adding anyway, "I hope so. I'd like to help this family out so they can get their lives back. I don't see any sign of a car following them. But you can bet he's around."

They finally pulled into a long driveway. Jonah looked around and shook his head. He walked over to the father. "Do you have a saw?"

"Yes, why?"

"Because all of these bushes under your windows is what make people like your perpetrator happy. They can hide under any of these windows. I see you have cameras set up all around the property. Anyone can get past those cameras and move from bush to bush without being seen. I'll cut these down while you show Kane through the house. Then I'll redo the security cameras."

"Okay."

"Can I help cut these down?" Martha asked.

"Sure, but stay close to me. We'll work on one bush at a time."

"Let's start on the bushes by my bedroom window first."

"Lead the way." Three hours later, they looked around the yard. It was a mess, but who the hell cared. "Tell me what this guy looks like. Unfortunately, I haven't been able to bring up a photo of him on my computer."

"I have a picture of him. I took it with my dad's phone and printed it out. I'll get it for you," she said before she ran off.

Jonah followed her into the house and went in search of the kitchen. He could smell food cooking. When he got there, he saw Kane cooking dinner. "Why are you cooking?"

"No one started dinner, so I did. I need nourishment."

"Mr. Brewer. Here is his picture," Martha said, running into the kitchen. "Mmmm, that smells good. I didn't know you would cook too. What are you cooking?"

"Spaghetti."

"Do they cook spaghetti in Scotland? I like your voice."

"Thank you, we cook everything in Scotland."

Jonah took the printout from Martha's shaking hand. Kane walked over, and both of them stared at the photo. Jonah took a picture with his phone and sent it to Brinley before sending a text. 'Can you run this photo, please? I'll owe you big time.'

"Yes, I'll do it now."

"He might have a different color of hair."

The guy had black hair. Jonah and Kane both knew it was dyed that color. Kane looked at Martha, "Has he always had black hair?"

"Yes, at least, I think so. You might ask my dad. He's worked for him for a while."

"I will. Where are your parents and your sister?"

"They are by the pool. My Sister Melissa has an issue with any kind of change. I think my mom wants us to stay in Melissa's room. That way, she won't have a bad anxiety attack."

Jonah walked to the back of the house where the trio sat and talked. He could see that Melisa was having a meltdown, so he went over there and sat down with them. "Tell me what the problem is?"

"Melissa can't sleep in another room. It's been tough on her since all of this began. I don't know if anyone will get any sleep if we don't try to figure out another way."

"How about if all of you sleep in Melissa's room?"

"No, no, no," Melissa said, crying.

"Well then. Why don't we do like my sister, Bird, and I always did? We'll camp in the living room. Do you have a tent?"

"Yes, we have a large tent in the garage," Greg said, nodding his head at the same time.

"How would you like that?" Jonah said softly, looking at Melissa.

"Yes, I would like that. I like camping," she whimpered, finally feeling hopeful for a less stressful night.

"Great, we'll set it up right now. Melissa, can you help to move the furniture around?"

"I'll start dinner," Dana said, with a relieved expression on her face.

"Kane already started. He's a good cook. We all know if we wait long enough, Kane will begin cooking. He's always hungry."

Dana smiled, "Then I'll help get all the camping stuff out and stay away from the kitchen."

"Why is your sister's name Bird?" Melissa asked, hurrying to keep up with Jonah. She grabbed his hand so he would slow down.

"Her name is Burdine, she didn't like that name, so everyone calls her Bird."

"I like that name. I want everyone to call me Mellie. Melissa is so long. Mellie is perfect."

"Mellie it is then," Jonah said smiling. They moved furniture around and put the tent up, and put air mattresses inside. Everyone got their sleeping bags and made the beds up. Mellie and Martha brought snacks to put inside the tent, and after dinner, they were going to make s'mores outside at the fire pit.

After dinner, the family went to bed without the s'mores. They must have been worn out. All of them were asleep as soon as they went to bed. Kane put on a pot of coffee and put cookies on the table. The lights were out. They didn't want to give the guy any lights in case he was outside watching.

"I'm going to go around the house and make sure everything is locked uptight. Save me some coffee and cookies."

Kane chuckled and nodded his head. Jonah had a sweet tooth and everyone knew it. His mind drifted, and she popped in his head before he had time to block her from it. He wondered how Julia was doing. It's been at least three months since he's seen her. He knew heartache. He dated Julia secretly for six months. She didn't want anyone to know about the two of them. Kane didn't like the secrecy. He was stupid and told her he loved her, she refused to see him again. Kane thought she felt the same way he did. He was wrong. She dumped him faster than he could take the words back. Sometimes he would remember their lovemaking. It was so much more than he's ever experienced before. He knew she felt something for him. Kane could feel it deep in his chest. Julia would never admit it, so he quit trying to get her to talk to him.

Jonah heard his phone ping and glanced at it. There was a message from Brinley.

'The man's name is Walter Pine. He's wanted for raping three young girls in Indiana. He's also wanted for the disappearance of an entire family. All I have to say is, 'Kill him.' He's no good.'

Jonah showed Kane the message. Kane shook his head. "The bastard is worse than we thought."

"It would seem so. I'll let the police know in the morning who we are dealing with. Have you called your sister?"

"Yes, but there is no answer. Rory is staying at the safe house with Austin. I'm sure she's fine."

Jonah shook his head. "I'm going to call Austin." The phone rang six times before it was answered.

"Hello."

"Rory, why are you answering Austin's phone?"

"Because he's in the hospital. I promised I would answer his phone for him tonight, but tomorrow I'm leaving it with someone else."

"Why the hell is he in the hospital?"

"Because his legs hurt him. First, they started tingling two days ago. Austin didn't tell anyone. Frankie was upset about that. I found him on the floor in his room. I had to close my eyes. He was completely naked."

"What the hell are you talking about?"

"Last night, I woke up because I heard something. It was Austin. He fell down in his room. That was the noise I heard. I found him. He was lying there in pain, as naked as the day he was born. I made him put his shorts on before I started his bath. Anyway, he's in the hospital because his legs are ready for him to use them again."

"Are you saying Austin is walking?"

"Not yet, but Frankie says he has to start therapy for his legs. He might be walking any day."

"That's wonderful." Jonah looked at Kane, "Austin is in the hospital. His legs are working again."

Kane stood up and quietly high-fived Jonah. "I knew he would walk again."

"Rory, did you give notice?"

"Yes, I gave a two-week notice. So you can stop worrying about me."

"I don't want you to go back there again. I have a feeling about that place."

"Jonah Brewer, I am not your responsibility, so please don't tell me what to do. Now, I'm busy answering Austin's phone. I don't have time to talk. This damn thing never stops ringing. I'm directing the Band on what to do. Rowan will be here to take over tomorrow. Good night, Jonah."

Jonah laughed. "God, I'm happy Austin is finally going to walk again," he said to Kane.

"What happened?"

"Rory found him on the floor." Jonah chuckled, "She said he was naked as the day he was born, and she made him put shorts on before she would start his bath. She acted like she was shocked at seeing a naked man."

"I'm sure she was. Rory probably hasn't ever seen a naked man. She would kill me if she knew I said this, but Rory is saving herself for her husband."

"What?" Jonah didn't know what to say. He didn't think he'd ever meet a twenty-eight-year-old virgin. Somehow that seemed to say back off. Jonah didn't go after virgins, and he wasn't going to start now.

"You act like you're in shock."

"I don't think I know any virgins."

"You probably do. You just don't know it. My sister made a promise to our grandfather, and she would never break it. So if you don't have good intentions, stay away from Rory. I'll take the first watch, you can get some sleep."

Jonah looked at Kane like he wanted to say something. Finally, he said. "You don't know what the hell you're talking about, so shut the hell up." He got up and left the room. But his mind wouldn't shut down. *Rory has never been with a man. Why do I care? I don't know. Or do I?*

7

Rory was at the hospital when Rowan and Piper walked into the waiting area. "Hello, you two. Where is the wee one?"

"She's at Brinley's. They'll bring her to us today. We'll be staying at the safe house for now. How is Austin doing?"

"He's grumpy because his legs pain him. But he's moving them as much as possible. He started therapy this morning. Here is his phone by the way," Rory said, handing the phone to Rowan. "It never stops ringing."

"It was a relief we had Austin taking care of the phones. Now we'll have to find someone to manage them. I'm sure Austin will want to be back out in the field working and not answering phones."

"How are you doing at the prison?" Rowan asked.

"I gave my two weeks' notice. Jonah has a feeling something is going to happen there. I believe in feelings."

"I've heard some crazy stories about that place. What made you decide to work there?"

"I needed something to do and I'm qualified so I applied for the opening and took the job when they offered it. Those men need to face what they have done, but too many of them refuse help, it baffles me. Instead of taking my help, they end up fighting with me, looking at me as the enemy. It's not worth my time. Plus, I was told there is some chatter about something that's going to happen."

"What do you mean something will happen?"

"I think they are planning a riot or something close to it. I don't think anyone there is safe around those monsters, but someone has to do the job."

"As long as it isn't you. I think you are making the right decision giving them notice."

Rory sighed, "Yeah, me too. I wish I could help them, but they have to want the help for themselves."

"I'm just glad you're leaving. Some people aren't worth your time. They'll die with the evil in them and that's just the way things end up I suppose. By the way, do you know when Jonah will be coming back?" Piper asked, looking at her computer. "We started landscaping the five acres behind his house, and I need him to walk back there with me."

"No, I don't know. I guess it depends on when they finish that job. If you don't need me, I need to leave. I have to finish my two weeks out."

"Go, we'll take care of everything from here," Rowan called out to her. "Rory, usually when there is chatter, there is movement. Be careful."

"I will." Rory hugged them and left. She was driving to work when her phone went off. Rory pushed the button and answered it, "Hello."

"Rory, this is Jackson. I realize you turned in your two-week' notice. I want you to be extra careful when you come in today. There is a lot of tension in the air. We have all the prisoners locked up, so you will have to talk to them through the bars." He took in a deep breath before adding, "I wish you could cancel your sessions for the next two weeks."

"I'm on my way. It'll be alright. If I feel like something is off, I'll leave."

"Okay, I'll see you when you get here."

Rory daydreamed as she drove. It was something she always did. At first, getting used to driving on the right side was tricky. She chuckled, remembering Jonah teaching her. Kane refused to teach her to drive because she screamed the first few times she saw a car coming at her. Rory learned fast, Jonah took her driving three times, and she had it down. Mostly because she wanted Jonah to be impressed with her. Rory wondered what it was about Jonah that she fell in love with. He isn't particularly nice to her. He isn't mean either. He treats her like he had to watch over everything she does. He constantly lectured her. He hurt her when he brought Evelyn to the bar-b-que and kissed her like they were going to take their clothes off. That made her angry which is why she left early.

He's never kissed her, and she knew this was the man she wanted for the rest of her life. What the hell was wrong with her? Rory was sure he didn't feel the same way as she did. He brought other women around, and he didn't care that she was hurt. He probably didn't even know she was. The only thing she could do was stay away from him when he had a lady with him. Or she would be hurting all the time. She still had some months here. Hopefully, something would happen before then.

She pulled into the parking lot and looked around. None of her homeless friends were there. She breathed a sigh of relief. Rory didn't want them injured if something happened at the prison.

"Hello," she said to the guard at the door.

"Hi, Rory. How are you doing?"

"I'm good. How is everything here?"

"It's nice and quiet at the moment."

"That's good."

"I hope it stays that way. Have a great day, Rory."

Rory smiled, "Thank you, you have a good day as well." She walked down the long corridor to her office. Her first patient was Nathan. She didn't mind him so much. He observed her more than he talked. A few times, she saw a smile in his eyes that would be gone in a split second.

A chair was set on the outside of the cells because of all the chatter going around. "Hello, Nathan. How are you doing?"

Nathan was angry, he whispered through gritted teeth, "Why the hell are you here? Don't you listen to what's going to come down? Stand up and go home. This place is not safe."

Rory could see the dread in his eyes but she wasn't going to let that get the better of her. She tipped her head and smiled. "Why are you here? You're not like the rest of these men. You have feelings, and you care. The rest of these guys have no feelings. You can look in their eyes and see no soul. Are you undercover?" she whispered and chuckled at the look that came over his face."

"You don't know what you're talking about. You damn right; these men don't have feelings. They sold their souls a long time ago. If they get their hands on you, they'll make you wish you were dead, and then you will be dead. So go home now before it's too late."

He stood up and told the guard he was finished talking. He wished he had access to a phone. He would make some phone calls.

Rory watched him walk away and shrugged her shoulders. She walked back to her office, and Jackson was there. "What's with Nathan? He seems upset. He wants me to go home."

"He's not like the others so maybe he's just worried about what they are planning. I came to tell you to be careful with

Mike. He'll hurt you badly before he kills you. Oh, yeah, a Jonah Brewer called. He wanted me to fire you today."

Rory chuckled. *Jonah might have feelings for me that he doesn't want to admit to himself. Don't start daydreaming about Jonah,* she scolded herself. *It will only lead to more heartache.* She looked at Jackson with dread. "Is Mike my next patient?"

He shook his head. "He's not going to be treated for the entire month. He's been causing a lot of trouble lately. You only have one more today, then you are finished for the day."

"Good, that means I can get out of here early. I'm going to the beach today. I've gotten myself a room on the beach, and my clothes are in the trunk of my car. That's one good thing about living here. I don't have far to go to the beach. Of course, these beaches here are entirely different from the wild beauty of Scotland's coasts."

"Are you staying the rest of the week there?"

"Yes, my brother is out of town. I don't know when he will be back. So I'm treating myself."

~

RORY WAS SLEEPING on the beach when she felt a shadow fall over her. She put her hand up and shaded her eyes.

"I thought that was you. What are you doing out here all alone?" Skye asked, carrying her surfboard.

Rory smiled and sat up. Skye sat on the lounge next to her. "I'm staying in that hotel behind me for the week. Kane is away, so I thought I would enjoy this beautiful weather. Are you surfing alone?"

"No, Dakota is still in the water." She turned and pointed at the woman standing on her surfboard. They both laughed when a large wave knocked her off her board. "You should have dinner with us. We do this once a month."

"Sure, I would love to. Are you sure you want me to barge in on your sister time with Dakota?"

"Yes, this time is for me to take a break from the little ones. Julia is watching them for me since Lucas is gone."

"Thank you for asking."

"Of course. We'll meet you at the hotel restaurant later tonight then."

"Are you two staying here?"

"No, I wouldn't stay the night from the little monsters. My friend is the hotel manager, and he lets us use a room to shower and change our clothes."

"Great, I'll see you in an hour."

"Awesome," Skye said before going back to where Dakota was.

I wonder if I could get an invite to Skye's home. I would love to meet Julia Sparrow, the woman my brother loves. Rory soon got up and walked to her room to shower and get ready for dinner. She was excited about having dinner with her friends.

8

It wasn't long after everyone went to sleep that Jonah heard the noise. It was only a soft sound, but he knew it wasn't natural. He tapped Kane on the shoulder, and they split up. There was no way the man could get to the family. Those rooms were blocked entirely off. For seven days, they waited for the man to show up. Now it would be over for the family. Jonah and Kane had already decided the man would die. They wouldn't let him live to rape and kill another person.

Jonah saw the shadow. He wanted to catch the man outside. Both he and Kane had their silencers on so they wouldn't scare the family. He saw the shadow at the same time Kane did. They slipped out through the window then shut it. The man meant business. He came with a machete in one hand and a gun in the other. Jonah took aim and called out the guy's real name.

Walter Pine aimed his gun. He was dead before his finger could squeeze the trigger. Kane called the police. Jonah went inside and woke the dad up to tell him they wouldn't have to worry about Walter Pine anymore.

"He's dead. The police are on their way. They won't use their sirens. I told them we don't want to scare the girls."

"Is it really over? Oh my God, he's dead. Thank you so much." Greg slumped down into the chair and cried. His wife Dana walked into the room. Her husband looked at her, "He's dead. It is over. We can get our lives back to normal."

"Oh my God, where is he?"

Greg looked at Jonah. "He's outside. The police are there now. We don't want to wake the girls. If you two need to see that he's dead, I understand. You can take a look. I'll stay inside with Martha and Mellie in case they wake up."

It took two days before Jonah and Kane were able to leave. It was a tearful goodbye for the family. They said they were going to camp in their backyard at least once a month, maybe more. Mellie cried the hardest. She didn't want them to leave. Martha wouldn't let go of Jonah's arm. He made them promise if they were ever in Southern California, they would call him. Finally, they boarded their plane and headed for home.

Jonah was anxious to see Rory. He couldn't get her off his mind. He's dreamed about making love to her. Why he would do that with her being a virgin, he didn't know. He didn't even know why he was in such a hurry to see her. He needed to get her out of his head. Before he did something stupid. He couldn't make love to her. She was saving herself for her husband. He wouldn't do that to her.

"You're quiet. Do you have something on your mind?" Kane asked after they were in the air for a while.

"I always have something on my mind."

"Do you want to talk about it?"

"No."

"Okay, I'll be right here if you change your mind."

"I have to tell Evelyn I don't want to see her anymore. The woman drinks vodka for breakfast. The real Evelyn didn't come out until the last couple of weeks. I'm not into women who have a drinking problem."

"Well, you haven't been dating that long, so I'm sure it shouldn't be that difficult."

"Say's someone who has never dated one woman longer than a week. When we were in the service, you had women hanging all over you. What's happened to that Kane Walsh?"

"He's still right here. He's learned not to let his heart become involved with anyone ever."

"Wait, are you telling me you've had your heart trampled on?"

"I'm not telling you anything. Besides, we were talking about you."

"We're through talking about me."

RORY WAS on her last day of work.

"Rory, are you ready for your last patient? How do you feel now that you'll be seeing the last of this place today?"

Rory smiled at Jackson. "I have to say I won't be sad leaving here." She turned when they heard a loud noise. "It's happening!" Rory shouted at Jackson. "Get out of here before they kill you!"

Before either of them could move, they were surrounded by at least eight prisoners. Rory didn't wait for them to come to her. She started kicking. She was always told to not let them have the first punch. Jackson was swinging. They locked the door then Mikey showed up. He kicked the door, and the wood splintered. Rory turned to Jackson. You have to leave. You have three wee ones that need you. Go out the window."

"We'll both go." He opened the window. "Rory, you go first."

The door crashed open. Rory looked behind her at Jackson standing at the window. She pushed Jackson through the window, and he fell to the ground. She threw her phone after him. Hopefully, he'll call the police. Rory kicked Mikey in the head, and he went down. She was fighting for her life. She heard someone roar and took a second to look. Nathan fought his way into where she was. She hoped he was going to help her. Rory wasn't sure she could handle him as well.

The next thing she knew, someone's fist hit her in the face. Rory almost went down. It took everything in her to stay on her feet. She heard someone shout her name, and Nathan was fighting next to her. Rory knew it was over. There were too many men there. She didn't know what to do.

"Go through the window, hurry, and get out while you can!" Nathan shouted.

Rory turned to get out, and she saw Nathan fall to the ground. She couldn't leave behind the person who helped her. She kicked one prisoner in the face and palmed another one in the throat. Someone grabbed her from behind. She elbowed him in the side, and another one hit her with something, and she blacked out.

When she opened her eyes, someone was trying to take her sweater off. Rory screamed as loud as she could and slugged him. He slapped her across the face. She heard someone making all kinds of noises. She turned her head and saw Nathan lying on the floor. He was bleeding from a head wound, and it looked like his nose was broken. She saw the hand that came toward her, and she kicked. Rory knew what would happen if these crazy bastards got her clothes off; every one of them would rape her. She had to keep her head on straight.

"Get the fuck away from me. What the hell do you guys

think you're doing?" She saw Nathan shake his head, but she ignored it. If she could get these horrible crazy bastards into a fight with each other, then maybe they would forget about her, and she could sneak out. *What the hell am I thinking? I'm as good as dead.*

~

Jonah had to call Rory; he needed to know if she was okay. This panic feeling wouldn't go away. "Hello."

"Hello," Jackson answered, his voice shaking uncontrollably.

"Who the fuck are you? Where is Rory?"

"I'm Jackson the Warden at the prison Rory works at. She is in trouble. She's in the prison with the prisoners. Some of them started a riot, and they have her. The stupid bastards said if we don't give them what they want, they'll kill her."

"You better hope there isn't a hair out of place on her head, or I'll string you up," Jonah growled.

Kane grabbed the phone. "If my sister is harmed in any way, I will kill every guard there."

"I don't have time to listen to this shit. I have to get Rory out of there." Jackson hung up the phone.

"Pull over," Jonah told the taxi driver. As soon as the car stopped, Jonah told him to get out. "I have to get to the prison before those prisoners kill Rory if they haven't already."

The driver panicked. Was this man being honest? Did he need to help someone or was he just about to steal his only means of income? He had no choice but to trust them, he knew for a fact he couldn't fight off both of them. "Fine," he said reluctantly, "but I'm going with you. I'm not leaving my car."

Jonah had four police cars chasing behind him before he

ended the chase at the prison. He and Kane were out of the car and ignoring the police. "Where the fuck is Jackson?"

Jackson stepped up, and Jonah's fist hit him hard in his belly. He went down.

"Tell me which room they are holding Rory in?"

"I think it is my office. I'll let you get by with hitting me this time, but only this time," Jackson whimpered from the ground.

They heard a vehicle come to a screeching halt, and turn to see Lucas Ryan jumping out. He looked at Jonah and Kane. "What the hell are you doing here?"

"Rory is in there."

"Fuck, what the hell is she doing in there?"

"She works here. Tell me what the DEA has to do with this place?"

"I have an undercover man in there."

"I'm going in," Jonah said, he turned to look at Kane, and he was gone. Jonah heard someone shout and saw Kane going inside. He hurried after him with Lucas by his side. The three of them stopped and listened. When they heard Rory scream, they ran down the hallway. Jonah kicked through one door. The other one was already broken in.

Jonah saw Rory fighting with three men who were trying to pull her sweater off. He went wild. He started punching all three of them, while Kane and Lucas took down the others.

Jonah picked Rory up and held her close to him. She sniffed a couple of times and then Kane took her from him. They started talking in Gaelic. He didn't know what the hell they were saying. But Kane was shouting, and so was Rory.

"No!" she screamed before she walked over and stood in front of the man on the floor. "He tried to help me. He wasn't in on any of this. So you won't touch him until he's seen a doctor."

By then, the police and everyone were inside. It was so

crowded Jonah put his arm around Rory and tucked her in close to his body.

She broke loose and walked to the man glaring at her. "Jackson, now you can go home and see your wee ones. Don't be angry with me for pushing you out the window. These guys came to kill you. I'll be leaving now. You should find a different job."

"I'm sorry I couldn't protect you. I'm going to miss you, Rory. I'm still angry you pushed me out the window, but I'm lucky you did. You take care of yourself."

"You too. Goodbye."

Rory turned to her brother. "I'm not going home. I'm giving him the three months I have left in this country to figure it out. If he hasn't, then I'll leave."

"What the hell are you talking about? You were almost brutally raped and murdered by these fuckers. I'm your older brother. You will do what I say. Look at you! They beat you! Your face is all bloody and swollen!" Kane shouted.

"I love you, Kane. I know this scared you. It scared me. I won't ever take on another dangerous job, I promise. Now stop shouting. My head hurts."

Jonah wrapped his arm around Rory. "Back the hell away from her. If you raise your voice to her again, I will flatten you."

"Can someone please drive me home?"

"We'll all take your car. We came by taxi." Kane looked at Lucas, "Pay the cab for us, and give him a big tip," Kane said, walking out the door. That's when they looked at the man on the floor. "Andrew." The guy opened his eyes and looked up at everyone looking down at him.

"Help me up." He was breathing hard and was sure he had some broken ribs. He looked at Kane, "Why would you let your sister work here? This is nothing but a fucking hell hole with the worse of, the worse." He looked at Lucas, "I never found out who the other guy was that helped Mike Reno kill all those people." He looked at Rory, "You are a hell of a fighter. We both would be dead if you couldn't do what you did."

"Thank you. I know who he is," Rory said. Her face was starting to hurt, and she felt like she needed to lay down. "His name is Scott. He's Mike's other personality."

"Are you sure?" Lucas asked.

"Yes, I'm sure. He came out one time when I was talking to Mike. He wanted to kill me. They should be in chains all the time. They are the evil devil."

Kane didn't look happy glaring at Jonah. "Why do you still have your arms around my sister?"

"Because she needs me to help her. Let's go. I'm running Rory by Frankie's."

"I don't need to be bothering Frankie. All I need is to soak in a tub and go to bed."

"Half of your face is almost as green as your eyes." Jonah bent his head and kissed her. He didn't know who was more shocked, him or Rory. He heard a growl, and the next thing he knew, Kane had snatched Rory out of his arms.

"I'll let you get by with that only because Rory needs help now."

"Would the both of you shut the hell up?" Andrew said. He looked at Rory. "I told you to quit this damn job."

Rory ignored him. She turned to walk outside. That's when she grabbed her side. The pain was horrendous. Jonah picked her up and carried her to the car. He sat in the backseat with her. "We'll let Kane drive."

9

"Frankie, I'm sorry. Jonah was becoming irritable, so I had to let them bring me to you."

"You need to go get a scan. I don't like this bruise on your side. I'll take the babies to Mama's and take you myself. I'm sure you are sick of listening to those two. What the hell are they arguing over?"

"Jonah kissed me and Kane is angry. Kane told Jonah he has someone to kiss, and it sure as hell isn't me."

"Ooh la la. What do you think about Jonah kissing you?"

"I loved it," she blushed. Kane wants me to go back to Scotland. He says it's too dangerous here for me. I have three months left before the time I gave myself to stay here expires. If Jonah doesn't realize he wants me to be his in that time, then I'll go home."

"So you like Jonah."

"I love Jonah. But don't tell anyone. I don't know why I love him, but there you have it. I do love him."

"So when he brings a lady around that must be very hurtful for you."

"Yes, it is. I feel like shaking Jonah sometimes. Or taking

everything into my own hands. I see the way he looks at me. I know he has feelings for me. He just hasn't done anything about it until today."

"This is going to be fun to watch. I'm rooting for you all the way. If you have to entice him a little just to give him a push, then do it."

"Like what?"

"When you go swimming around Jonah, wear a skimpy bathing suit. I mean, you have this beautiful curvy figure. Show him what he's missing," Frankie said, pointing to Rory's body. "Just show it off more than you usually do. I wore an outfit made of scarves. It was beautiful and very provocative. Storm has me wear it sometimes so he can take it off." Frankie giggled, and her face got bright red.

"When the bruises go away, I'll do that."

"No, do it now. Put it on while you still have the bruises. Jonah will feel protective and realize how close he came to losing you."

"Frankie! I would never have thought your mind could be so conniving," Rory laughed. "We'll stop on the way back from the hospital."

"You two can leave now. I'm taking Rory to get a scan and see if she has any damage inside this one bruise. Frankie lifted the edge of Rory's shirt up. I don't like the looks of this one."

"I'm going with you," they both said at the same time.

"No, she'll feel uncomfortable if you come along. She wants you to stay behind."

Jonah looked at Rory, "Is this what you want?"

"Yes. Frankie will drop me off at the safe house. I'll stay there until Missy gets back."

Kane shook his head. "You call me if anything shows up on the scan."

"I will. I'll see both of you later today."

Rory could tell Jonah was going to argue. "I'm sure everything will be okay. Don't worry about me. I'm as tough as old nails. You know what they say about tough as nails."

"No, I don't know what they say. Tell me."

Rory shrugged her shoulders, "I don't know either."

Jonah stood there he couldn't believe she would think he wouldn't worry, "You've got to be fucking kidding me. What do you mean, don't worry about you? You were attacked by a bunch of animals who almost raped you. They would have murdered you if we hadn't shown up, and you tell me not to worry." He saw Rory shudder, and he put his arms around her. "I'm sorry, I won't say another word. We'll see you when you get to the safe house."

Rory nodded and turned toward Frankie, "I'm ready." Someone knocked on the door at the same time. It was Frankie's mom to watch the babies.

"While you have your scan, I'm going to go visit Austin," Frankie said.

"Tell him I'll come by before I leave."

"He might be going home today. If he is, he can go with us."

"That would be wonderful. Will Austin have a therapist coming each day?"

"Yes. I'm sure Austin will be complaining really loud. Every step of the way."

Rory went with the technician, and Frankie went to see Austin. She stopped when she entered his room and saw Jonah and Kane. "I thought you two were going home?"

"Austin called us for a ride home. We knew he would get his legs back to working. How is Rory doing?"

"She's getting her scan."

Austin shook his head, "I can't believe she was still working there. She told me that she gave notice."

"She did," Kane said, "today was her last day."

Austin shook his head. "You don't take care of your sister. So from now on, I'll take care of her. I'm going to let you know, Kane, I'm going to start pursuing Rory. She is amazing. I'm already walking. I'm going to take her to dinners and the movies. I would consider myself lucky to have her in my life."

"The hell, you will. Rory is mine. Stay away from her."

Austin looked at Jonah, "Yours, what happened to Evelyn?"

"I don't have Evelyn in my life anymore."

"Have you told her that?"

"I will tell her today. So back off. Rory is mine."

"I'm not going to argue with you, Jonah. I'm surprised you are thinking about Rory as a girlfriend. You've never thought of her like this before. You've always brought other women around. You didn't think of her feelings while you were making out with those women. You might want to be with Rory, but I doubt that she wants to be with you."

"Well, see. Are you ready?"

"Yes."

Frankie stood there listening. She couldn't wait to tell Rory. "Well then, this was interesting."

"Yes, it was," Kane said. "Don't tell Rory about this conversation. I'm going to straighten both of these men out."

"I didn't hear anything. My lips are sealed."

10

"Austin, how are you feeling? Look at you. You look so handsome. It did you good getting away from here, away from that damn ringing phone."

Austin shook his head, looking at Rory, "Me, how are you feeling? My God, have you seen your face? Let me see your side?"

"You don't need to see her side," Jonah said. "Rory, you should get some rest."

Rory ignored him. She was angry with him anyway. She heard him on his phone telling Evelyn he would see her in an hour. "I hurt some, but nothing inside was damaged. I'm glad I don't have to go back there to work. I feel bad about people having to work in places like that. When I went to college and got my degree, I admit I didn't think about the people I would be trying to help. I think I'll stick with painting murals. It's something I enjoy."

"Don't forget my offer. I would love to help out. I'm going to be out of commission for a while anyway."

"That would be great. I'm going to start painting Bird's

children's murals. Plus I'll be finishing soon. As soon as my body heals a little, we can start working."

"Sounds good to me."

"What are you talking about?" Jonah asked from the doorway.

"Didn't I hear you tell your girlfriend you would see her in an hour? You better get going," Rory said, trying to keep the hurt from being heard in her voice.

Austin heard it, though. He tried changing the subject knowing Rory couldn't hide the hurt much longer. "So, whenever you want to get started, let me know."

"She isn't my girlfriend. We went out a few times. I'm going to tell her it's over, that's why I'm meeting her. I want to tell her face to face."

Rory didn't want to hear it.

"Rory, I'm not with anyone. Go get some rest."

Why do I care so much? One little kiss that's all I've ever had from him, just one little kiss. "Yes, I'm off to bed. Thank you, Frankie, for being there for me again."

"You're welcome. Call me tomorrow."

"I will. Good night." Rory went up to her room and took a shower, then she crawled into bed naked; that's how she liked to sleep. She was asleep as soon as her head touched the pillow.

Jonah heard the screaming. He jumped out of bed. He knew Rory was having a nightmare. It was the third one tonight. She had kicked her blankets off and was crying. He covered her up and pulled her into his arms, saying soothing words to her until she calmed down. He laid her back on the pillow and was at the door when he heard her speak.

"Please stay with me tonight. I'm scared. I know I'm only dreaming, but if you were here, maybe I wouldn't dream."

"Kane won't like it."

"He doesn't need to know."

"I'll sleep on top of the blankets."

"I can put something on."

"I'll sleep on top of the blankets."

Rory scooted over so Jonah could have room. She waited until he got settled, then she went to sleep.

Jonah wasn't as lucky. He fell asleep when the sky was turning light. So when Kane checked on his sister, he found both of them sleeping. Rory had her naked leg over Jonah's body, while she had her head on his chest. He counted to ten before saying something. He poked Jonah on the shoulder.

Jonah's eyes flew open. He saw Kane and rolled his eyes. The last thing he needed was a lecture from the big brother. He put his finger to his lips and gently lifted Rory off his chest. She moaned in her sleep and got right back on his chest. Jonah looked at Kane and shrugged his shoulders.

"She kept crying out with nightmares. What was I supposed to do? She was scared," he whispered. "I'll let myself out in a minute. You can start the coffee."

Kane didn't like it but he left. He would give Jonah thirty minutes, if he wasn't downstairs by then, he would drag him down.

As soon as Kane went out the door, Jonah looked at Rory. Her face was about five different colors. He still wanted to roar with red hot anger when he thinks about those men almost raping Rory. He wondered when he admitted to himself how he felt toward her. He didn't want to let her know yet. He had to do it slowly so as not to scare her. She wasn't used to men. He couldn't just come out and claim her as his. He touched his lips to her lips real gently. Jonah sighed. He would go slowly with Rory. But he would make sure Kane and Austin knew she was his woman. Austin was going to have to back away from her. He climbed out of bed, almost humming to himself. Jonah went across to his room and got dressed. When he went downstairs, Kane waited at the bottom of the stairs.

"What the hell is going on with you?"

"Nothing is going on with me. Is Austin up yet?"

"Yeah, he's with his physical therapist."

Jonah looked at the clock and was surprised it was already eight. "Look, Kane, because you're Rory's brother, I'll tell you this. And I will only say this once because it's none of your business. I didn't say anything to you about you and Julia." Jonah held up his hand when Kane was going to interrupt. "Yes, I knew. Rory belongs to me. She doesn't know it yet, but she's mine. I'm going to take it slow with her. I don't want to scare her off."

"Why would you think it would scare her off if you didn't take it slow?"

"Because she isn't used to men."

Kane laughed so hard he had to sit down. "That's the funniest thing I've heard. Rory has dated lots of guys."

"But you said she's…."

Kane held up his hand, "She still dated men."

Jonah got himself a cup of coffee and picked up the paper. There was an article in there about what happened at the prison. It said they moved one of the prisoners a Mike Reno, to a mental facility. He hoped they had the guy chained tight so he couldn't escape. Jonah lost his breath. He had a feeling go through his body. He picked up his phone and called Bird.

"Good morning, is Granny around?"

"Good morning to you too, brother dear. Yes, she's right here. Are you coming to dinner Saturday?"

"Yes. I will be there."

"Good, here's Granny.

"Granny, how are you doing?"

"I'm doing very well. Thinking of buying a home here. I

want to be with my family, and Bird needs me to help her with all these kids. Now, tell me what is wrong."

"I'm not sure anything is wrong, but I have that feeling."

"You have my blood running through you. So if you have that feeling, then you follow it. You've gotten this feeling since you were a child, and you know it's right most of the time. So that means you are in love."

"Why the hell does it mean I'm in love?"

"Because it works with someone you care about."

"Yes, care about, but I never said anything about love. I have the same feeling with my buddies I work with." Jonah heard his granny and Bird laughing. He shook his head, "I'll see you both Saturday.

"Good morning, Jonah."

Jonah raised his head and smiled, then he frowned. "What the hell are you wearing?"

"My swimsuit. I'm going swimming."

That's not a swimsuit. It's a damn shoestring. Austin and his therapist are outback. They'll see you." He walked to her and looked at her side. My God, I wish I would have killed those bastards. This must be so painful." He touched the bruise.

"I have to go," Rory turned and walked out the door. She had to get away from Jonah before she confessed her love to him. Having him with her last night made her want him more. When she looked out her window and saw the handsome hunk helping Austin, she hurried and put her new swimsuit on and ran downstairs. She was going to make Jonah jealous. Now she didn't think it was such a good idea.

Jonah watched as Rory walked to the pool. All of that beautiful body of hers on view for those men to look at. He heard her giggle and turned to the other people in the backyard. Austin's therapist was drooling. Jonah watched as the man left Austin's side and walk to Rory. He looked at her bruise, and then he put his hand on the bruise on her side. Jonah may have growled because everyone looked at him.

"Don't you think you should get back to your patient and get your hands off of my woman?"

Austin coughed, and Kane laughed. Rory smiled to herself. The guy jumped back and almost into the pool. He watched the tall muscled blond man coming toward him, and he hurried back over to Austin. "I'm sorry. It was all professional. Please don't think I would try anything with your wife."

"I'm not his wife. I'm not even his girlfriend. Her name is Evelyn. What is going on with you, Jonah?" Rory's words were harder to understand. She wanted to cry because Jonah said she belonged to him. She was so happy. She wouldn't give him the satisfaction of getting by with saying it to someone else before he said it to her first.

Jonah took his shirt off and put it on her, then he took her hand and walked her inside away from all those eyes and ears.

"I'm sorry I said it like that. I wanted to take it slow with you. I want to take you to dinner and everywhere. I know this is crazy, but I've never felt this way before. I love you. I know that's shocking news. I tried fighting it, but when you got attacked I didn't want to wait anymore."

"You love me. You don't know me."

"I've known you for over a year. I didn't know that I loved you that long, but I know it now."

"You were at your girlfriend's last night."

"All I did was tell her we were through. I haven't been intimate with Evelyn in a while."

"You two were all over each other at Willow's bar-b-que. I was there, I saw the entire disgusting thing."

"That was not me. It was Evelyn. She has a drinking problem. She said she's going to get some help. If you had kept watching, you would have seen me untangle myself from her. I took her home. I'm not with her anymore. I only want to be with you. Can we at least see what might come of us?"

"Yes, we can."

Jonah pulled her to him. He wrapped his arms around her and gently kissed her busted lips.

Rory wasn't having any of that. She wrapped her arms around him and got as close to him as she could while she deepened the kiss.

"Is this how it is?"

"Yes. I want you to kiss me like you love me every time."

"Do you have anything to say to me?"

"I think I might love you too. But I've known about it for a long time."

"I'm sorry it's taken me so long to say something. Now, can you go change out of that shoestring and put some clothes on?"

Rory smiled. "I will this time, but it's the only time you can tell me what to wear."

Jonah chuckled, "I can't promise that."

11

Rory was busy with painting the newborn's room at Bird's house. She decided that since this would be her new business, she would treat it as such. Austin helped sort the paint colors some of these paints old and Rory wanted to toss them she only wanted to use the finest quality of paint. Bird knew what she wanted, and she wanted beautifully painted scenes with gorgeous colors. She drew a photo for Rory, who was studying them right now. "This job was going expensive, and she couldn't make any mistakes. Have you ever painted anything like this?" she asked Austin. Showing him the picture.

"No, I have no talent with those kinds of things. Have you done anything like this before?"

"Not like this, but I have painted things on wood before. This will take some work. I'll have to study this before I start. First, I'll draw it myself. That way, I can size it right without messing anything up." She stared at the drawings a little longer. "When do you have to be back?"

"I can't stay today, but I can come back tomorrow. Is Kane getting the keys for his house today?"

"Yes, I'm so excited. They will deliver the furniture next week. Kane's going to paint his rooms this week. I'm so glad I'm busy. I don't like painting house rooms. I would rather do the kind of paints I do."

"Me too. As soon as I can walk normally, I'm going to Texas to check on my ranch and to see my family."

"That should be fun. You're almost walking normally already. Is it painful?"

"No, it's just that sometimes my leg buckles, and I don't want my dad to see that."

"You don't want him to worry because he doesn't like your job."

"How did you guess?"

"You told me before he didn't like it and when you were a detective he wanted you in Texas at your ranch. I guess no matter how old you get, you are still your parent's child, and they will always worry about you."

"Yes, I'm sure they do. I know I will always worry about my children."

"Yes, me too. I can't wait to have wee ones like Bird has."

Austin chuckled, "Bird! She has a new one every year. Shoot, I have an appointment in an hour. I got to go."

"Yes, and all those babies have so much fun together. Drive careful."

Austin thought Rory looked sad. "You okay? How are you and Jonah doing?"

"We are getting to know each other. The thing is, Jonah doesn't kiss me anything like he kissed those other women I've seen him with. He kissed them long and deep. I could tell he wanted them by the way, he held their bodies rubbed up against his. He barely kisses me. I don't know what the problem is. I'm thinking he doesn't enjoy kissing me like he did those women."

"Maybe he doesn't want to rush you."

"Yeah, that's probably it. I'm going to measure the three bedrooms at Bird's home tomorrow. Do you want to go with me? It was two murals now it's three."

"I have therapy in the morning. I'll be available around ten."

"Ten it is then. I'll pick you up."

As soon as Austin was in his vehicle, he called Jonah, "Hello, Jonah. Why do you not show Rory how much you care for her? She said you barely kiss her. She told me she's seen you kiss other women, and you never kiss her that way. What the fuck Jonah? If you don't want her, then don't lead her on."

"If you must know, I'm taking it slow, so I don't scare Rory. Austin, stay the fuck out of mine and Rory's love life."

"She doesn't want you to take it slow. She wants you to kiss her like you love her, you idiot."

JONAH MISSED SEEING RORY. He promised himself he would take it slow so as not to scare her. But it was more challenging every time he saw her just to keep his hands to himself. He stepped out of the shower and dressed. Maybe Austin was right. Perhaps he would show Rory how much he loved her. He smelled food cooking and went in search of Kane, who was in the kitchen cooking. They all knew Kane had his meals at a specific time, and if no one started cooking, then Kane would cook for everyone. "Where are the ladies?"

"They are watching the telly."

Jonah walked into where the elderly ladies sat, watching a game show. "Hello, ladies. How are you doing?"

"We were wondering when we would get to go home."

"Do you want to tell me why you are afraid to be in your home?"

"No. I don't think so." They had nothing more to offer.

"Dinner will be ready soon." Jonah couldn't get anything out of these three sisters. He stopped and thought before he took his phone out. He pushed a few numbers into it and waited. "Hello, sweetheart," Jonah said as he walked to his room.

"Jonah, I miss you."

"I miss you too, baby. I wanted to see if you could do me a favor. I have three elderly sisters here we're guarding. They are hiding from their nephew, but they won't tell me anything. I wanted to see if you could come here and talk to them. I'm sure they'll talk to you. Everyone talks to you. What do you say?"

"I have to go to Bird's tomorrow and take some measurements. Maybe I can call her and put it off for a couple of days. Then I need to call Austin and let him know I'm not going to Bird's."

"Why do you have to call Austin?"

"Because he's helping me do Bird's home."

Jonah frowned, "I didn't realize he was helping you do the painting. So I can tell Rowan he can bring you here?

"Yes, when will Rowan be here?"

"In about ten minutes."

"What? I need to get busy and pack an overnight bag."

"I'll see you when you get here, darling."

"Okay, bye Jonah."

~

RORY MADE her calls and packed her overnight bag. She decided tonight she would kiss Jonah the way she wanted him to kiss her. Her doorbell went off, and she opened the door. Rowan stood there grinning.

"Hi, are you ready?"

"I'm ready." She locked up Missy's house and walked out to the car. "Tell me about these sisters who are afraid of their nephew?"

"We don't know much. They have been very secretive. All we know is they say they're scared their nephew might harm them."

"Sounds like someone planted a thought in their heads. I'll get to the bottom of this."

"Are you happy you'll see Jonah?"

"Yes, I miss him. What do you think about Jonah and me?"

"Well, I think the two of you are perfect together. I knew both of you wanted each other. I'm glad Jonah finally acted on it."

"Really, it's strange for you to say that."

"Why is that?"

"Jonah doesn't even kiss me like he loves me. He's not once tried to make me his."

Rowan was suddenly becoming a little uncomfortable with this conversation. "Why don't you talk to him about it?"

"I'm going to do more than that. Tonight Jonah will either take me to his bed, or I'm going home to Scotland."

"Good luck."

Rory chuckled, "I'm sorry. I am so used to talking to Scottish people I forget Americans get all uncomfortable talking about certain subjects."

Rowan smiled, "We're almost there."

"You mean it's this close to the safe house?"

"Yep, two miles. This is another safe house. We are starting to acquire quite a few safe houses. Here we are."

Rory got out of the vehicle just after Rowan did. They walked up to the door. It was opened right away and Jonah pulled her into his arms and kissed her like he's never kissed her before.

"Excuse me, you're blocking the entrance," Rowan said, standing behind them.

Jonah chuckled. He took her hand, and they walked where the ladies sat watching the television. "Ladies, this is Rory Walsh. Rory, these lovely women are Katherine, Lucy, and Betty. I need to check on dinner. Can you three entertain Rory for me? Take good care of her. She's my lady."

"Yes, we will. Hello Rory."

"Hello, it's nice to meet you."

"Oh, are you from Scotland?" Lucy asked. "I love listening to Kane when he speaks. Your voice is so lovely to listen to."

"Yes, I am. Kane is my brother."

"Your brother, that's wonderful the two of you are here together."

"Yes, I didn't want Kane to be here with no family. But now he has lots of friends."

"Are you and Jonah in love?" Katherine asked, leaning forward.

"I love Jonah, but he doesn't treat me like he did his other girlfriends. I watched him with them. He kissed them like he wanted them. He hasn't kissed me like that."

Katherine shook her head. "Well, you should take control. I wish I would have done that. When I was younger, I loved Benjamin Baxter so much my heart has never healed. He is the only man I have ever loved. We were to be married. Benjamin was on his way to my house, and the train went off the cliff. It almost killed me. I went to the wreck site and hunted for my love. I would have done anything to have had his child. I don't care if I was scorned by the town. I still love that man to this day. If you love Jonah, you go after him."

"I'm so sorry for your loss," Rory offered, seeing the pain in her eyes as she spoke. "I plan on doing that tonight. I want

Jonah to kiss me like he loves me. Not like he has to kiss me. I want someone who wants to tear my clothes off and make love to me…" Rory pulled herself back from her reverie, "I'm sorry," she was flushed. "I got a little carried away. Why are the guys guarding you ladies?"

Betty looked around so no one would hear her. "Our nephew is going to kill us so he can take all of our money."

"That's horrible. Has your nephew always been after your money?"

"Oh, no, dear. Brett has his own money. He has been taking care of our finances forever. My brother took care of it before he passed away. Brett took over."

"Is he a mean man?" Rory whispered.

"Oh, no, he's the sweetest young man. He loves us, and he treats us like we are very special to him."

"Then why do you think he's out to harm you and take your money?"

"Well, our pastor has convinced us…"

"He hasn't convinced me," Lucy interrupted.

Betty gave Lucy a dirty look, "As I was saying, our pastor is worried about us. He said he would take care of us."

"Did you sign over power of attorney to your pastor?"

"Yes, he had the papers all drawn up. All we had to do is sign the forms."

"Will you excuse me please…?" Rory went to the doorway and called, "Jonah, can you please come in here."

"Hey, love, what is it?"

Rory looked at the ladies, "A shark dressed as a pastor has talked these women into giving him power of attorney. He convinced them that their loving nephew who treats them with love and respect is going to kill them."

The three sisters started crying as soon as the words left Rory's lips. Katherine blew her nose and wiped her eyes, "What have we done, sisters? That man has turned us against our loving nephew. Oh, my. He has taken our money. Will Brett ever forgive us?"

"Give me your nephew's phone number. We need to call him right away," Jonah said.

"Do we have to bring Brett into this mess?"

"Yes, we do. The pastor has power of attorney over your money."

"Lucy gave him the phone number, and Jonah called him. "Hello, is this Brett Anderson?"

"Yes, it is. But I'm in the middle of a family emergency, so I can't talk right now."

"Would that emergency have anything to do with your aunts?"

"Yes, who is this?"

"My name is Jonah Brewer. I'm with the Band of Navy Seals high-security team. We've been guarding your three aunts for two weeks now. It would seem their pastor convinced them that you were going to kill them and take their money. So they signed over power of attorney to him."

"Fuck, the pastor has already been arrested. I thought for sure he killed them. I've been so scared. My aunts don't have money. My grandfather made some bad investments. My father has always provided for them. We never let them know they were broke, so please don't mention it. I'll have someone pick them up. Can you give me the address and put my aunts on the phone, please?"

Jonah put the phone on speaker. "Ladies, your nephew would like to speak to you. You are on speaker so he can hear all of you."

All Brett could hear was crying. "Hello, Aunties. I have a car coming to pick you up. Don't worry about your pastor. He has been arrested. It would seem the man has taken a lot of money from people at your church. He won't be bothering you anymore. I love you. I will see you at dinner tomorrow. Bye, Aunties. I love you."

"I'll help you pack," Rory offered.

"What about dinner?" Kane asked.

"We'll get something when we get home. Thank you, gentlemen, for taking such good care of us. I'm sure the driver will be here soon. We only live a few miles from here."

"Why don't we eat before we go home," Rowan suggested, "I'm starving."

"I'm staying here tonight with Jonah. I'll help him clean the place up."

Kane narrowed his eyes, Rowan smiled, the ladies giggled, and Jonah looked scared to death.

12

"Are you sure this is what you want to do? Kane asked his sister for the tenth time. I don't want you upset down the road."

"I said I was going to help clean everything up. I didn't say anything else. Now, stop asking me these questions. Go with Rowan. I know what I'm doing. I'm twenty-eight. I'm a big girl."

Kane shook his head and walked out the front door. "Is he finally gone?" Jonah asked, putting his arms around Rory.

"Yes, Jonah, I want you to make love to me like you love me. Not like you can barely stand to kiss me."

"Is that what you think, love?"

"Yes. That is exactly what I think. I've seen how you kiss women, and you don't give me what you gave them."

Jonah took her hand and walked with her to his bedroom. "That's because Kane told me you have never been with a man. Quite frankly, I've never been with a virgin. I didn't want to scare you off. But never doubt that I want you. It's been the hardest thing I've ever had to do, keeping my hands off of you. Tonight is for us. I'm going to show you how much I love you. I want you to tell me if I'm going too fast."

"I won't be telling you anything. I want you to treat me like you do any other woman."

"I will be treating you like I love you. I've never loved another woman. You will be my first love and my last." He took her face in his hands and kissed her like he's never kissed a woman. He would never kiss another woman again. This was his woman, and she had all of him.

Rory had chills all over her body when Jonah lifted her top over her head. Then he unbuttoned her pants and slid them down her legs. He backed her up to the bed. They both went down. His lips found hers, and he devoured her. Rory knew this was right. She wanted to give herself to the man she loves and Jonah was the only man she would ever love.

"How are you doing, sweetheart?" he asked between kisses.

"I'm doing fantastic."

He raised up and pulled his shirt off. Rory forgot how large he was. He was all male, muscular, and handsome. Rory knew Jonah was all hers, tonight, and forever she was all his. Rory almost died when his hand slipped inside her panties. He had those off of her before she could take a breath.

"Are you still okay, sweetheart?" he whispered in her ear.

"Yes, fantastic," Rory whispered back. Jonah's mouth found her breast. She cried out, but it was the most beautiful feeling she's ever felt. His mouth left her breast and made its way down her body. When his tongue found the inside of her thigh, she raised her body. And a noise of pure pleasure came from deep in her throat. When his mouth touched her, Rory cried out. She ran her hands up his sides and felt abdominal muscles quiver. She liked the idea of him quivering from her touch. She ran her hands down his back and under his boxers.

"Rory," Jonah growled, "if you don't want me to embarrass myself, don't put your hands much lower, sweetheart. I'm holding back all I can right now."

"Why are you holding back?"

"Because I want you ready for me when we join."

"Jonah, I am ready."

Jonah chuckled; he raised up and kissed her, then his hand lowered. He moved her legs apart until he touched her. His finger gently went inside. All he could think was he is the first man to ever touch Rory, the first to make love with her, and he would be the last. The love that came over him brought tears to his eyes.

Rory was freaking out. She was so damn ready for Jonah to take her and make love with her. She was bucking. It felt like she would burst. "Jonah, do something."

"Let it come, sweetheart."

Jonah didn't know how he was going to hold back from making Rory his. He was ready to explode. He raised himself over her, dipped his head, and his lips locked with hers as he gently entered her. "This might hurt a little my sweetheart, but only this one time, I promise."

"I don't care, Jonah, just do it. I don't want to wait any longer. Rory pushed up as Jonah pushed down. There was a slight burning, but Rory didn't let that stop her. She met Jonah with every thrust. Until she felt like something was going to happen, she raked her hands all over Jonah's back as her body orgasmed time after time. Rory was crying when Jonah came deep inside her.

"Are you okay, baby?" Jonah asked, kissing her all over her face.

"Yes," she moaned, sounding out of breath as she sniffed, "that was so beautiful."

Jonah chuckled, "It was better than beautiful. I've never felt like this. I love you, Rory."

"I love you too. Jonah, ye are mine now."

"As you are mine."

"Can we do it again?"

Jonah bent and kissed her, "Are you too sore?"

"Na."

"Are you sure?" he asked, kissing her like he loved her.

"Jonah, yes, I am sure. My body is burning for you."

Jonah chuckled. They made love until the wee hours. They fell asleep and didn't wake up until the ringing of Jonah's phone woke them. "Hello." He watched Rory raise as she threw her leg over the bed. Jonah took her hand and shook his head. "Kane, we are cleaning the house. We'll be home this afternoon. I have to wash all the bedding."

"Where is Rory?"

"She's around here somewhere." Jonah smiled and winked at Rory. *God, she's beautiful.* "I'll have her call you. Bye, Kane." Jonah pulled Rory under him. He bent his head and kissed her. Rory could feel his body hard against her. She was so ready for him. Jonah lowered his body, his arms bracing above her. She looked up into his eyes, and he wondered if she would shut her eyes or turn her head away. Jonah would wait until she looked at him. Rory grabbed the sheet with both of her hands. Then she put her hands on Jonah and ran her fingers over his body. Rory reached her hand down and touched him. Jonah inhaled a sharp breath.

"Let's do that tonight."

"Are we going to be together tonight?"

"Baby, we're going to be together every night. Then he slipped inside her. Rory wanted to cry. She had no idea it would feel like this. They came together as one, and Rory met him with every thrust. When she orgasmed, Jonah released himself inside her. She felt like she had no energy.

Her legs felt like rubber. But she knew they had to get up. "I'm going to take a shower."

"We'll take one together. I'll show you how to make love in the shower."

Rory chuckled, "That sounds like fun."

"Oh, sweetheart, it's way more than fun," he said in the sultriest voice he could muster.

~

THEY WERE in the kitchen eating. The house was clean, and the bedding was all washed. They heated up leftovers before heading home. Jonah was nervous asking Rory this question. He didn't know what she would say. "Rory, do you want to live with me? I have a home in Temecula. I have a huge barn you can set your shop up."

"You want me to live with you?"

"Yes, I want you with me forever. I love you. You know that."

"Yes, I know that."

"What's wrong?"

"I don't know what Kane will think about me living with you."

"Who cares what Kane thinks? We love each other. I want to wake up with you every morning, sweetheart."

"Let me talk to Kane. I want him to understand how much I love you. I don't want him to think I broke my word to my grandfather."

"Rory, don't let him talk you into not being with me."

"I won't. Nothing could keep me from you. Ye are the man I love. Forever!" Rory said as she took his hands and squeezed them. A tear slipped from her eye. "Whit's fur ye'll no go past ye." Rory knew he didn't understand her. "What's meant to be will be," she translated.

Jonah nodded his head and kissed her. "I love you. You

belong to me. Rory Walsh, will you marry me and become my wife?"

"Ye want me for a wife?"

"Yes, did you not know that? I would never have taken you to bed if I didn't want to marry you."

"Yes. Yes!" Rory shouted and threw her arms around Jonah.

Jonah ran his hands in her hair and brought her mouth to his. He plundered her lips as he pulled her as close to him as he could get. "I will never hurt you. I will guard you and take care of you and our children. I will cherish every minute we have together."

"Let's go back to bed," Rory said. She could feel his hardness throbbing against her body.

Jonah picked her up and carried her to bed. They stayed there the rest of the night. Early the following day, Rory declared she had to go to Bird's and check on the progress of the construction work. "First, let's go tell Kane we're getting married. Then we'll tell Bird. I hope she's happy for us."

"Are you kidding me? She loves you. Everyone loves you. They'll all be happy for us."

13

Kane stopped talking when Jonah and Rory walked into the kitchen. He was cooking lunch and talking to Rowan and Killian. Rory had a massive smile on her face. "I know you are bursting to tell me something. What is it?"

"Kane, Jonah asked me to marry him!"

Kane smiled and hugged her. "I'm happy for you, and you too, Jonah. Do you want me to call Elspeth and ask her to get everything ready in Scotland? Have you picked a date?"

"No. Slow down. Ye are not planning my wedding."

"I'm sorry, I'm just happy for you."

"I know. We haven't discussed a date." Rory looked at Jonah.

"One month. Call your sister, she can come here. We will get married in my backyard. Piper has been landscaping it. I wanted it to be perfect for you."

"Did you landscape your backyard for me?" Rory asked, putting her arms around him and kissing him. She laid her head on his chest. "Thank you."

"Is your backyard big enough?" Kane asked.

"It's five acres."

"You had five acres landscaped for me?"

"I wanted you to feel like you were in Scotland. I knew I was going to ask you to marry me, sweetheart," he said, looking down into her face. "I just didn't know if you would say yes."

Rory gave him a long hot kiss, just like she loved him. Until her brother wouldn't stop clearing his throat.

"Congratulations, you two. I'm happy for both of you.

"I'll call Bird. She'll want to help you with the planning," Killian said, hugging Rory, and shaking Jonah's hand.

"I'll call Piper," Rowan said, hugging Rory and shaking Jonah's hand. "Congratulations."

"Thank you. I'm so excited. I have to get back to work. Is Austin here?"

"He's in the pool."

"I'm going to go tell him we're getting married. Then I need to go to your house, Killian, and take measurements."

Jonah had his arm around her. He knew Austin had feelings for Rory. He wanted to make sure Austin knew she was his. "Rory, I'll drive you. I want to show you my house," he said, walking with her to the backyard.

"Okay. Rory saw Austin lifting himself out of the pool. Then it dawned on her that he would be perfect for Elspeth. He could help her with the farming. What could be much different between cows and sheep? She turned toward Jonah and smiled.

"What?"

"I'll tell you later," Rory whispered. "Hello, Austin. We wanted to tell you, Jonah and I are getting married."

For a slight moment, a wave of jealousy washed over him, but Austin had to admit that they were right for each other. "Congratulations, you two. When is the big day?"

"In one month, I have to call my sister and make sure she has someone to take over on the farm for her."

"You have a sister?"

"Yes, Elspeth. You'll meet her at our wedding. Do you want to help me with some of the painting tomorrow at Bird's house??"

"Sure, you can count me in. I have therapy in the morning, but I'll see you after that."

"Thank you. I'm going to try and get as much done as I can before the wedding. I'm going to Bird's right now, and then Jonah is taking me to see his home. So we'll see you tomorrow."

"Yes, I'll see you then."

"What are you hatching?"

"Don't you think Austin would be suitable for Elspeth?"

"I don't know, Elspeth. I don't think you should try matchmaking for Austin. He loves his job, and his ranch in Texas is vast. He's not going to move to Scotland. So, given that Elspeth wants to stay in Scotland, I suggest you stop thinking about what you're thinking right now."

"You're right. I don't know what I was thinking."

Jonah, Killian said before they walked out the front door. "We leave at four in the morning for Maine. There will be four of us going. Don't be late."

"You don't have to worry about me. I'm never late."

"Damn," Rory said, walking outside. "You have to go away."

"It won't be for long. I'll be back in no time." Jonah pulled Rory into his arms and kissed her. He nuzzled her neck, while she melted in his arms.

"Ummm, I'm glad you decided to make me yours. Does that mean we can make love any time of the day?"

"Yeah, sweetheart. As long as we are alone. And here

comes Zane." Jonah straightened. He raised as Zane walked up to them with a big grin on his face.

"Well, you two look like you are enjoying the day."

"We are at that," Jonah said. "Rory and I are going to be married in one month. We hope you and Polly can be there."

"Are you kidding me? Why that's fantastic news. Congratulations. I can't wait to tell Polly." He hugged Rory and shook Jonah's hand. "Our group is growing every year."

"Yes, it is," Jonah said, laughing. "We are on our way to Temecula. I'll see you tomorrow."

"Okay, see you tomorrow."

"My granny is at Bird's house. If she acts strange, it's because she is strange. I don't know how else to explain it to you."

"Hey, I was born and raised in the land of fairies, believe me. I've heard it all before. You don't have to worry about Granny around me."

"Do you have many relatives left in Scotland?"

"I have lots of cousins. They live in a castle. All of them are very wealthy. I will have to invite them, or their feelings will be hurt. My grandpa and their grandpa were brothers. Their brother was the elder brother, so they have the castle. My grandpa bragged about how he was the winner because he didn't have to maintain the castle. Mostly I knew my cousin, Callum. He lived with us for a while. I'm sure he's back at the farm. Callum worked on the farm with Elspeth after he got out of college. My cousin, Duncan, thought he threw his college education away. They argued about it all the time. When grandpa died, he moved out. I heard he is traveling around the world."

"Why did he leave?"

"I think he wanted the farm. It has four ponds and a beautiful forest. There are waterfalls it's beautiful. The farm is massive. The house is over eight hundred years old. It's not quite a house. It's more of a small castle. It's been updated, of course. There are one thousand acres with sheep and horses."

"It sounds magical."

"It is. One day we will go there. My ancestors believed there were fairies on our land. So you see nothing anyone says seems strange to me."

"Yes, we will. Didn't you want the farm?"

"I enjoyed working on the farm while I was there with my grandfather. If I had the farm, I would have to ask my husband to change his name to Walsh. Only a Walsh can own the farm.

"If your husband loved you as much as I love you, he would change his name."

"I'm glad I didn't have to ask that of you. Then you would be Jonah Walsh," Rory chuckled.

"Yeah, I think I would like to keep my own name, but I would do it for you," he leaned in and kissed her.

14

Rory took measurements in the newborn's room. She was doing this room first because the baby would be here soon. Bird's house, "This is going to look great. Did Bird say when she'll be back?"

"She should be right back. Her granny wanted to get a cake to celebrate something. She said if you show up to ask you to wait for her," Dave, the contractor, said.

Jonah pulled her into the other room and pulled Rory into his arms. "How about if we come back later? I have a powerful feeling to get you alone right now," he said, backing her up against the wall and nibbling her ear.

Rory wanted to melt into the floor. She wrapped her arms around him, and Jonah picked her up. Rory wrapped her legs around him. Her sundress going up around her hips while Jonah tucked his hands under her bottom and held her closer.

"We need to get out of here," Jonah whispered in her ear. That's when he heard a noise. He shut his eyes for a brief second before raising his head. "Hello Granny, hello Bird." Then Kelly ran past him. "You're gross." Jonah chuckled and put Rory down. He straightened her dress out before stepping aside so his granny could meet her.

Rory didn't want to raise her head. She was so embarrassed. *Why can't the damn floor open up and swallow me whole?*

"Rory, how are you doing?" Bird said, grinning.

Rory raised her head and burst out laughing, "I was doing fantastic, and then ye interrupted us."

Jonah chuckled and pulled her into his side. "This is my granny."

"Hello, Granny. I'm pleased to meet ye."

"Granny, Bird; Rory and I are getting married."

Bird threw her arms around Rory and then Jonah. "I'm so happy for you both."

"That's why we went and picked up a cake for you two, so we can celebrate with you," Granny said, hugging them.

"Don't ask how she knew. Sometimes Granny knows these things. Jonah said, chuckling.

"Killian called and told me," Granny said, shaking her head at Jonah.

"We are having the wedding in a month in my back yard. You two can help us with everything." Jonah turned and looked at Rory, "Isn't that right, sweetheart?"

"Umm, sure. I wouldn't even know what to do, without some help. Who do I call? I'll have to have a company for catering and one to set everything up for the wedding. We need chairs and tables. I'm so busy right now. I think I'll be staying at Jonah's while he's away on his new case." She looked over at Jonah, "Is that okay?"

"Of course, we'll bring all of your things. It's going to be your home also. Why don't you call and see if Elspeth can come early? She can stay with you until I get back."

"She stays so busy on the farm, but I can ask her. Maybe she will be able to come a week early."

"Let's have some cake before you two have to leave. I can

tell you are anxious to be home," Granny said. Bird giggled. Rory felt her face burning. She looked at Jonah, and they both chuckled.

"We'll take our cake to go. We have a lot of *planning* to do," Jonah said, grinning.

"Bird, I'll have the baby's room painted before the wedding. I want you to have your kitchen finished. Then we'll finish the other rooms."

"I can't wait to see the outcome. I know they will be beautiful. But I don't want you putting this before your wedding."

"I won't. I can do both."

"We'll see you two later. I'm going to show Rory where we'll be living. Come along, darling," Jonah took Rory's arm and pulled her along with him.

"Welcome to the family, Rory," Granny called out as the two exited the house hastily.

JONAH PULLED up to his home, watching closely for Rory's expression. You could see all the trees in the backyard from the driveway. Piper did a fantastic job. The five acres were beautiful. Rory was the first person besides Piper to see it. Rory got out of the car and walked to the back gate, she opened it, and Jonah could hear her indrawn breath. Rory ran through the trees laughing. She saw the bridge and the hidden seating with beautiful throw pillows. There were dainty, colorful flowers everywhere. When she turned to Jonah, tears were falling from her eyes.

"Did you do all of this for me?"

"Yes, I want you to like America, so you will stay here. If I could bring Scotland to you, I would. This is the closest I could get."

"You didn't know if we were going to be together at that time."

"But I knew I loved you."

"We are going to make love right now on this soft grass," Rory said, pulling her dress over her head.

Jonah watched as she slipped out of her panties and threw her bra into a tree. He laughed while walking toward her taking his clothes off. They made love until the sun started going down. "Do you want to see the inside of your home, sweetheart?"

"Yes. I hope it has lots of bedrooms," Rory said, walking into her new home. She stopped and smiled. The house was beautiful. Every room was perfect. There were four bedrooms, but Rory didn't let that worry her. They could always build onto the house. "It's perfect. I love this house. Did you do all of the remodeling yourself?"

"Austin helped, and a couple of other professionals."

"It's beautiful. I love my new home. Show me where our room and shower is located," Rory said, standing naked in the room.

"I kind of like the grass stains on your bottom." Rory turned so he couldn't see her bum. He reached for her and carried her into their room and into the shower. They made love in the shower until Jonah heard Rory's stomach growl. "It's time to eat. I'll cook you a meal on the first night in your new home."

15

Rory's phone would not stop ringing. Austin looked at her, "Aren't you going to answer the damn thing."

"I need to get this door finished. Elspeth will be here tomorrow, and I only have a week before the wedding. I haven't even bought my dress yet, so I don't have time to answer my phone every time it rings."

"Go buy your dress. I'll finish up here."

"I am not going to leave for you to finish this," she laughed. What made Bird decide to have the children's table painted?"

"It's because she wants their playroom painted. She wants the table to match the room."

"Thank you, for helping me. I'll go shopping when Elspeth gets here. We call her Elie. She hates shopping. But she'll go with me…" before she could finish talking, her phone rang again. "Alright, I'll answer. Hello, who is this?"

"Hello, Rory. This is Jackson."

"Jackson, is something wrong?"

"They put Mike Reno in a mental prison hospital. He

killed the nurse and broke out of the hospital with some others. The doctor there said he told everyone he was going to kill you. I think you need to be guarded until he's caught."

"That poor nurse. I hope they catch him soon. How many other people have to die before they catch him?"

"Rory, did you hear me? He's coming after you."

"I heard you, Jackson, but I'm not afraid of Mike. Did you forget I can take care of myself? He doesn't even know where I live."

Austin was listening to everything Rory said. "Give me the phone," he said, holding his hand out for it.

"Hello, this is Austin Sawyer. Tell me what the hell is going on."

"Mike Reno escaped from the prison hospital for mentally deranged prisoners, and he said he was going to kill Rory."

Austin looked at Rory, "We'll take care of it at this end. Can you email me everything you have on Mike Reno?" Austin gave him his email address.

"Gladly."

Austin hung up the phone and handed it back to Rory. "I'm going to call Jonah and tell him what's going on. He can come back early. They are going to be wrapping everything up there anyway."

"Austin, I don't want you to say anything to Jonah until he gets home. Then I will tell him what Jackson said. I don't want to bother him with my problems." Rory turned back to the table and didn't notice Austin walking outside and taking out his phone.

"Hey, Austin, what's up?" Jonah answered. He asked Austin if he would watch over Rory. So that's what he's doing. Jonah needed to know what the hell was going on.

"The warden called and told Rory that Mike Reno killed a nurse and broke out of the mental hospital prison with some others. He has been telling everyone he's going to kill Rory Walsh."

"That fucking bastard. I'll kill that son of a bitch if he gets anywhere near Rory. Austin, don't leave her side. I'm leaving right now. I'll see you tomorrow. Is Rory with you now?"

"Yes."

"Put her on the phone, please."

Austin walked back into the barn on Jonah's property, where they had moved all of the construction work. "Rory, Jonah wants to speak to you."

Rory took the phone from Austin. "Hi, Jonah. Are you coming home soon?"

"Rory, I want you to stay close to Austin. Yes, I'll be home tomorrow."

"I have to pick up Elie tomorrow. I guess Austin can take me. Jonah, you know I can handle Mike Reno. I don't want you to worry. I'll keep Austin with me the entire time."

"Good, I'll see you tomorrow, sweetheart."

"I can't wait to see you! I love you so much."

"I love you too, darling. Bye."

"Bye Jonah, have a safe trip." As she handed Austin back his phone, her phone rang. Rory picked it up. "Hello, hello." She shrugged her shoulders and laid it back on the table. When it rang again, she ignored it. When it stopped ringing, she turned it off. There were things she needed to finish, and the phone ringing slowed her down.

They worked until the sun went down. Rory called a halt and picked up her phone. She had missed fifteen calls. All of them from the same number, when she called the number back no one answered. *It must have been a wrong number.* They locked up the barn and walked toward the house.

"Who's that?" Austin asked, reaching for his gun and realizing he didn't have it on him. "Go back to the barn and lock yourself in there," Austin said under his breath.

"Why?"

"Something is wrong. Go back to the barn. Now!" he ordered her through his teeth.

Rory was debating on what to do when she saw three men walking toward them. "I'm staying with you."

"Fuck, listen to me. These men aren't here for anything good. Please do as I say."

Rory wasn't sure if they had a gun. They were still too far away for her to see who they were. Then she heard a noise behind her and that crazy laugh. Both she and Austin spun around. They couldn't see anything. When Austin shouted and fell to the ground, she saw the Taser prongs stuck into his skin. *What am I going to do?*

"Run Rory!" he winced.

Rory saw Austin jerking and knew they kept hitting him with the Taser. She saw crazy Mike Reno, with a Taser gun in his hands. "I'm surprised you only brought five men with you. Don't you remember the last time we were together?"

"Yeah, I remember I was about to get myself some, and your boyfriend stopped me. He's nowhere around here now." He hit the Taser again, and Austin jerked.

"You fucking bastard, I'm going to kill you."

Mikey laughed when he looked at Austin. "How are you going to do that?"

When he pushed the button again, Rory kicked it out of his hand. She kicked him in the face, and he was laid out flat on the ground. By then, the other men surrounded them. Rory braced herself for a fight. She saw Austin trying to get up but was having a problem with his leg. She blocked him from the men. "What are you men doing here?"

When one of the men went to kick Austin, Rory kicked him so hard he went flying backward. Then she was tasered. She cried out and tried to get it out of her skin. And it went off again. Austin jumped to his feet and plowed into the men.

That gave Rory a chance to get the Taser out of her skin. She saw Mikey get up, and she tripped him by sticking her leg out. She jumped up and knocked two guys down. She watched another two take off running.

"Get back here; are you all fucking chickens!" Mikey shouted.

The sirens surprised Rory, but it scared the hell out of the others as all of them took off running.

"I'll see you again, Doctor, so you better watch your back."

Rory went running after them, and Austin pulled her back. "Let's get in the house before they realize that siren is not coming here."

"Can you walk?"

"Yes, I can. How are you?"

"My skin hurts where I pulled that Taser out. They must have taken them from the hospital."

"Do you think they are all from the hospital?"

"Yes, I could tell by the clothes they wore. I need to get my gun from Kane. I'll have him bring it to me."

They made it into the house, and Austin went straight to his gun. We're not staying here. He called the police and it wasn't long before they showed up. Austin called Jonah. Rory heard him shouting from across the room. "Will you stop shouting? You need someone else guarding Rory. My leg gave out on me. She would be with those men right now if she didn't know how to fight."

"No, I don't want anyone else. I'm not having anyone else," Rory shouted.

Austin looked at Rory and had to chuckle. "You don't have any say in this. I can't keep you safe. My leg proved that."

"You were tasered in your leg. The bastard kept shocking you. That has nothing to do with you guarding me."

"She's arguing right now. How the hell can I tell her

anything? She won't let me get a word in. Here, he wants to talk to you," Austin said, holding out the phone to her.

"Hi Jonah, before you say anything, Austin is my bodyguard. The only reason he couldn't get up was that he had the damn Taser in his leg. It has nothing to do with his leg giving out. They kept pushing the button so it would send a shock into his leg."

"Are you alright?"

"Yes. It's only where the Taser got me that I hurt, and that's because I pulled it out." She wasn't expecting the noise that came over the phone. She dropped it and it cracked the glass. She looked over at Austin. "Sorry, I wasn't expecting him to start shouting in my ear."

They could still hear him shouting. Austin picked up the phone, "Why are you shouting?"

"Take Rory to Arrow's house. They won't know where she is until the police catch all of them. Austin, don't leave her side. I'm counting on you to keep her safe."

"Did you not hear me when I said I can't keep her safe? My leg gave out on me. It's not entirely healed."

"That's why you're going to Arrow's. Put Rory back on the phone."

"You owe me a new phone," Austin said.

"Rory, Jonah wants to talk to you."

"Tell him I'm staying here. This is my house, and I'm not letting those men in here to destroy it. No, I'm not going anywhere. Jonah, you can't tell me where to go. I'm a grown woman." She said loud enough for him to hear. She shook her head and took the phone.

"Please go to Arrow's house until I get home. I'll worry all night about you."

"I'll be fine. You can't watch over me twenty-four hours a day. You have to trust me when I say everything will be fine."

Rory looked out the window and saw the police cars. "I have to go. The police are here. I love you."

"Rory, wait..."

"Whoops, dang, I hung up on him," Rory said out loud as she opened the front door.

Austin walked out and went to shut the door; Rory put her hand in the way but he stopped her, "Rory, you can stay inside. I need to talk to the police."

"I should talk to them as well. Mike Reno was my patient. I need them to understand how dangerous this man is. They need to go through all the homes around here to ensure he's not hiding in them. Or has not killed the families."

"I'll make them understand. You should go take care of your side. You're bleeding."

Rory looked down, and blood was everywhere. Her blouse was soaked and torn. She went inside and let Austin talk to the police. She took a shower and bandaged her side, then she went in search of Austin. He was cooking dinner. "What did the police have to say?"

"They're checking all of the homes around here. Why don't we eat and then relax? You must be exhausted with all that fighting."

"I'm okay." Rory yawned, "Maybe just a little tired."

Austin put a plate of scrambled eggs and bacon in front of her. "Here, eat this, then get some rest."

Rory heard someone at the door and jumped.

"That will be Arrow, and a few others will be here tonight. That way, you can get some rest, and you won't have to worry about anyone showing up later tonight."

Rory was relieved there would be more guys there. She finished her meal then went to her room. Tomorrow Jonah will be here, and so will Elie.

16

Jonah walked into the bedroom and saw Rory sleeping peacefully in their bed. He'd been awake all night trying to get to her. He stripped out of his clothes and crawled into bed with her. She was beautiful. She was sleeping in one of his shirts. He slipped his hands up under the T shirt and pulled her to him.

Rory smiled, Jonah was home. "How did you get here so fast? Umm, that feels good. I missed you so much. What time is it?"

"It's three in the morning. Raise up so I can get this off of you. Rory raised up so Jonah could take the shirt off. Before she knew it, she was lying naked next to him. "I missed you, baby."

They were facing each other. Not an inch separated them. "I don't think I like you going away for so long at a time. The next time I'll go with you."

"Okay, I'll take you with me the next time," he whispered between kisses. "You'll soon be my wife. Where I go, you go."

"Yes," she moaned.

Jonah turned her on her back and kissed her. He kissed

her like she was the only woman in the world for him. He kissed her like he loved her. "I love you so much, sweetheart. I'm going to keep you safe. I'm so sorry I wasn't here with you when those bastards came to our home."

"You can't be with me all the time. I understand that. I can take care of myself."

"Darling, I know you can, but you don't have to. You have me. Forever." He bent his head and kissed her neck, and made his way down her body.

They made love until the sun was coming up. Jonah had fallen asleep. Rory got up and showered. She had to pick her sister up at the airport. She quietly made her way downstairs and out the door. She climbed into her vehicle and headed for the airport with no one even knowing she left. Until Jonah came downstairs looking for Rory. He looked at the clock and couldn't believe it was eleven.

"Is Rory in the barn?"

Austin looked at him like he was crazy, "I thought she was with you. Surely, you haven't already lost her." They both heard the door shut and women laughing. Rory walked into the room with a woman who was her identical twin. Except Elspeth had long hair while Rory's was short.

"There's two of you," Austin blurted out, staring at them.

"Yes! Elie, this is Austin Sawyer. Remember I told you he saved my life. And this is Jonah Brewer. The man I'm marrying."

Elie hugged Jonah, "I'm happy to welcome you to our family." Then she turned and looked at Austin, "Have we met before?"

"No."

"I feel like I know you."

"No."

Elie walked to him and hugged him. "Thank you for saving Rory."

"Rory saved me."

"Austin, you know that is not true. Let's go make some coffee," Rory said and took Elie's hand.

"Rory, why did you leave the house without telling anyone?" Jonah said, walking with her.

"Because you were all sleeping. I didn't want to bother anyone."

"You have a crazy man out there wanting to kill you, and you don't want to wake us. I swear to God, Rory. What am I going to do with you? Don't leave the house without Austin or me."

"Okay, don't sleep so sound next time. We are going to go shopping for my dress after I fix us something to eat. Who wants to go with us?"

"Don't please me so much and I won't sleep so sound," Jonah bit back. Rory blushed hearing this. Jonah smiled. "I'll go. Austin needs a break. So how come I didn't know Elspeth was your identical twin?"

"I thought everyone knew." Rory looked at Austin. He hadn't said anything. He was still staring at her sister. "Are you two hungry?"

Jonah went over and kissed Rory. He pulled her into his arms. "I missed you the entire time I was gone. I'm starving. What about you, Austin?"

"What?"

"Are you hungry?"

"Yes, I'll fix us something."

Rory smiled and shook her head at her friend Austin, "I'm making us something to eat. We'll all go into the kitchen and talk while I make lunch."

Jonah chuckled and walked past his buddy and slapped him on his shoulder. "Let's go to the kitchen." Jonah saw Austin shake his head.

"So, Elspeth, you raise sheep on your farm," Austin said as he gazed at Elspeth.

"Please call me Elie, all my friends do. Yes, I raise sheep. I had hoped Rory would come back home to help me, but she has fallen madly in love with Jonah. I miss my sister." Elie turned her head and looked at Rory, "Who wants to kill you?"

"One of my patients from the prison was put into a mental prison hospital and broke out. He killed the nurse, and five men with him also broke out. They also showed up here. Thank goodness I had Austin here to save me."

Austin looked at Rory like she was crazy. "What are you talking about? You saved yourself."

"You're so modest, Austin." Rory looked at Elie, "He was my bodyguard while Jonah was away."

Jonah knew what she was doing. She was trying to do some matchmaking, and he told her not to try and mess with people's lives. He would talk to her when they were alone.

"So Elie, do you visit America often?"

"No, this is my first time. I don't usually take long trips. I've been to England, that's it. I love where I'm from and I have everything I want there. I enjoy hiking and camping in the open when I have free time. I like being outside and having the sky for my roof. Have you always lived in Los Angeles?"

"No, I have a ranch in Texas. I haven't been there in a while. I've been laid up for a few months. I'm fine now. I plan on going there after the wedding. I couldn't miss my best friends getting married."

"Hmm," Elie watched him, "I feel like I know you. I wonder why I feel that way. Have you been to Scotland?" instead of waiting for him to answer, she asked for his hand. "Can I see your hand?" She lay her hand on the table palm up and waited for Austin to put his hand in hers. Jonah and Rory watched to see what Austin would do.

Austin didn't want to put his hand in hers. He knew it would tingle. His body was still experiencing some of the tingling from the hug she gave him. He took a breath and laid his hand in hers. Sure enough, he could feel the tingle throughout his body.

"Do ye feel that?" Elie asked with a catch in her voice. "My skin is tingling. Can ye feel it?" Elie looked like she found a bit of magic.

"No, I don't feel anything," Austin lied.

Jonah knew he was lying, and so did Elie. Jonah couldn't figure out why he would lie about it.

"Are ye sure?" Elie asked. She smiled at Austin. "That's okay. You don't have to say anything."

"Well, I think I'll go back to L.A. I have some projects I have to take care of. I will see you in a couple of days." He looked at Rory, "I hope they catch those bastards. You don't be going in the backyard alone."

"I won't. I thought you were staying here until after the wedding?"

"I was going to, then I remembered I had so much to take care of. I'll be leaving for Texas right after the wedding." He stood up and hugged Rory goodbye. "Take care of your side where the Taser prongs clamped onto you."

"I will. Thank you for helping me with everything. So, should I tell Bird we'll finish the table and walls when you get back from Texas?" Rory felt terrible for Austin. He actually looked like he wanted the floor to swallow him up.

"Damn. No, don't tell Bird that. I'm going to the barn right now. I'll see you later today." He got up and walked out the kitchen door.

All three of the ones left behind in the kitchen stared at his back. "He felt it. It must have scared him," Elie said.

"I believe you're right," Jonah said. "So, what was it?"

"It was a tingle that went through my entire body. It was almost like a shock that went through me. I wonder if he has some kind of electricity in his body."

"Maybe it's just something between the two of you," Rory said, pretending to pick some lint from her sweater. Of course, he did get shocked from that Taser."

"Whatever it is, it won't go any further than right here. I have a sheep farm in Scotland that I will never leave. Austin has a cattle ranch in Texas. The only thing we could get out of this is a few nights of joy."

Rory busted out laughing, and Jonah choked on his milk he'd just taken a drink of. "Are we going to get our rings when we go to town?"

"I have the rings. There is a place in Scotland where we live the man who owns the shop makes one of a kind rings. I bought mine and my husband's rings when I was twenty-one."

Jonah pulled her out of her chair and sat her on his lap. "This is why I love you so much," he said and kissed her.

17

Jonah walked into the barn where Austin was sanding down the table for Bird's home. "Why did you leave so fast yesterday?"

Austin looked over his shoulder, "If I had stayed another minute in the kitchen, I would have taken Elie right there on the table. I've never felt anything like that before in my life. My body had a shock going through it, and it went straight to my dick. I knew if I ever had Elie, it could never stop at one time. She would have to move here, and I know she would never do that, so I left."

"Damn, you passed that up. Elie told us she would have enjoyed having a few nights of sex with you."

"What? Fuck, why would you tell me that? It's weird she is identical to Rory. I think I'm better off going to Texas and finding Cathy. She'll keep me up all night."

"She really isn't identical to Rory. If you listen to them talking, you'll see they are different. Elie has been around people more than Rory. There are other things I won't point out to you. She's coming to help Rory with some painting. Apparently, she also knows something about paints."

"Damn, I hope she doesn't want to touch me again."

"Why is that Austin? You don't like the sensations going through you," Elie said, walking up to him. "Let me just do a test. I've never felt that sensation before either." She looked into his eyes, stood on her tiptoes, and let her lips touch his.

Austin shut his eyes, made a noise in his throat, and pulled Elie up against him. He didn't come up for air for a while. Then, when he did raise his head, he kept kissing her in small kisses. It seemed his lips couldn't get enough of her. Elie never opened her eyes until he stepped back. Then he had to hold onto her so she wouldn't fall. She had a tear that fell onto her cheek, and Austin wiped it away, before he bent his head and kissed her some more.

Rory didn't know what she was supposed to do. She looked at Jonah, and he had a massive grin on his face. She took his arm, and they walked out behind the barn. "I don't think Elie should have done that."

"I bet Austin is glad she did. Follow me, sweetheart, let's go back to bed."

"Stop that. I have to finish this table. I'll count to twenty, then I'm going back inside."

Jonah chuckled, "I have some lawyer work to finish up. I'll be in my office if you change your mind."

Rory walked back inside the Barn and walked over to her table, where her tools were. She started working before looking around to see where Elie was. She didn't see her or Austin. *Where are they*? Rory shrugged her shoulders and kept on working.

Jonah came to the barn and looked around. "So they're gone."

"Are they not at the house?"

"No. Austin's vehicle is gone. They must have left together. Were they here when you came back in?"

"No. I wish one of them would have left me a message."

"Have you checked your phone?"

"No." Rory picked up her phone and saw a message from Elie. "She says she's with Austin. They'll be back later today. She's sorry she couldn't help me with my work. Can you believe that? They've only ever said one word to each other. Do you want to help me load this table? It goes to Bird's house. The contractors are finished working on her family room. I can't wait to see it."

"Yes, where is the truck?"

"It's backed up to the back of the barn. We'll go through the back door. This barn is way better than the shop my grandpa had. He would have loved this barn. That is if you could have gotten him on a plane. He's like Elie in that he never flew in an airplane. Elie has flown a couple of times. But she doesn't like leaving Scotland. I think Elie's afraid it will change or something. She doesn't enjoy driving in a car. She would rather walk. We always walked everywhere."

"I can't wait to see where you lived. We'll go after you finish Bird's murals. Why don't we take a honeymoon there? Then we can go to a few more other places across the ocean."

"That would be wonderful. I have so many places to show you. We will have a blast. Jonah, I can't wait to be your wife. I love you so much."

"You are the best wife any man could have. I count my blessings every day for your love. I know you will be a wonderful mother to our children. I love you, sweetheart."

"Let's go take a nap."

Jonah bent his head and kissed Rory. "I am a little sleepy." Jonah threw his arm around her shoulder, and they walked toward the house. The men came out of nowhere. Guns pointed at their heads. Jonah pushed Rory behind him before he reached for his gun. He shot two men in the head. From the corner of his eye, he saw Rory flipping through the air. She kicked a man in the face, and he fell back. Jonah ran to help her when a bullet stopped him in his tracks. He stopped and looked down. Blood poured from his stomach. He looked at Rory, and she was looking at him. He saw her screaming, but he couldn't hear her. Jonah fell down. Rory ran to him.

"You bastards. What have you done? Jonah, darling, please don't die. Please, please, don't die. A man was pulling at Rory. You fuckers leave me alone," she screamed.

"Get her. We'll have fun with her before we kill her."

Rory stood up. She looked Mike in the eyes. I'm going to kill you. Do you hear me? She shouted. Rory charged him. She kicked him so hard she heard his neck snap. He screamed, and she kicked him again. Die, you fucker. She saw the other two. Their guns were pointed at her. She didn't care. She would kill them before they could kill anyone else. Rory felt the bullet tear through her back. She turned and saw another man running toward her with his gun pointed. Rory reached for Jonah's gun and fired. The man fell in front of her. She swung around, and it felt like her body ripped in half. She fired the weapon, and one man screamed as he ran away. The other man pointed his gun at Rory, she felt the bullet hit her head, but her weapon had already fired and hit him between the eyes.

~

STORM AND FRANKIE rang the doorbell, and no one answered. So they walked around back, and Frankie screamed as she ran to Rory. She called nine-one-one. She looked over at Jonah. Storm was checking to see if Jonah was breathing.

Frankie was crying so hard she could hardly see she couldn't find a pulse on Rory. It looked like she had a bullet in her head and one in her back. "Is he breathing?"

"I feel a slight pulse, I think. I don't know. Where is the damn ambulance? How did this happen? Is Rory alive?"

"Barely. She has a bullet in her back, and her head got hit with a bullet. I don't think it is in her head, though. Even though her skull is cracked. Hell, I don't. I need help here. Let's work on one at a time. First, call Kane and tell him he needs to come here. I wonder where her sister is." Then they heard some voices. "We're back here," Storm shouted.

Kane and Marc came around the side of the house. Both of them stopped before going into action. Kane was on his knees next to his sister, and Marc was at Jonah's side.

"What the fuck happened?" Kane asked. Kissing Rory. "Rory darling, we're right here. Listen to me. I want you to try with all you have in you to live. Jonah needs you to live. He's going to live. Marc is over there right now shouting at him. Frankie is stopping the bleeding in his stomach. So you don't have to worry about him. Can ye open your eyes lass or something to let me know ye hear me? Let me check this wound. It looks like the bullet didn't penetrate your skull. You're going to be okay, sweetie. I'm here now."

The ambulance showed up at the same time the police did. "Who wants to tell us what happened here?"

"When we got here, we found Jonah and Rory like this. The dead men must be the ones who broke out of the prison hospital," Storm told the police.

"We were called out here once because someone was after Doctor Walsh. Apparently, they came back. And by the looks of it, they lost. So how are Doctor Walsh and Jonah doing?" the police officer asked.

"They're barely hanging on. I don't know what's going to happen. We can only pray they make it to the hospital. Their wedding is Saturday. Marc, I'll follow you to the hospital. Frankie is riding in the ambulance. Kane, you can ride with me," Storm said.

Kane had his back to the people so no one could see his tears. He couldn't lose his sister. He loved her so much. Your siblings weren't supposed to die so young. Why wasn't Austin here? "I wonder where Elie and Austin are. I'll try calling them again. I can't believe this happened to Rory and Jonah. God, I hope they live. I don't know what to do. I feel like I'm standing here doing nothing. I heard Frankie telling the ambulance driver that Rory was shot in the back. So they had to be careful in case it hit her spine."

"Yeah, I heard the same thing. I'm glad they killed those bastards. I wish they would have saved me one." Storm looked over at Kane, "How are you doing?"

"I'm in shock. I can't believe this happened." He wiped his eyes, "Jonah and Rory both might die. I can't wrap my brain around this. I can't get a hold of Elie. She must be with Austin. I can't get a hold of him either. Has anyone called Bird?"

"Frankie talked to Killian. They'll meet us at the hospital."

18

Kane paced the halls of the hospital, waiting for his sister and Jonah to get out of surgery. The surgeon said even though the bullet didn't penetrate Rory's skull, it is the reason she's unconscious. It must have hit so hard that her brain was jarred hard enough for her to blackout. Kane looked up, and Julia stood in front of him. He blinked so she wouldn't see his tears. He wiped his hands across his face. Julia walked up to him and put her arms around him. Kane buried his face into her neck and allowed the tears to fall.

"Why are you here?"

"I wanted to come and be with you. Tell me what the hell happened."

Kane scrubbed his hands over his face. "I guess those fucking escaped criminal mental patients showed back up. This time they had guns."

"Are you saying those men were there once before, and only Jonah and Rory were there this time? Why wasn't anyone else there with them? Did they not think the killers would come back?"

"I don't know. Elie, my other sister, is in town somewhere. She came for the wedding, but I haven't been able to get a hold of her or Austin."

"Let's go get a cup of coffee. Do they know how long the surgery will be?"

"No, they don't know anything yet." Kane looked over at Julia. She had her dark, luxurious hair up in a ponytail. Her beautiful blue eyes looked at him with concern. How he missed her. He would give anything to take back those three words. I love you. It scared her off. "How have you been doing, Julia?"

"You know me, I always manage to get myself into trouble."

"Tell me about it. It'll take my mind off of Rory and Jonah."

"I doubt this is any better, but let's see if it will help as you say. I may have killed a man who was trying to sell his children. I was working undercover when a man came upon me asking if I wanted to buy his kids. He said I can take all four of them for five hundred dollars. He then took four small toddlers from his car, naked. The bastard was selling them for sex. Babies, the oldest, was probably five. I gave him the money because I knew he would sell them to someone else. Then I took them to a friend's house until I could finish my job. I saw the man later that night. He was shooting up. I got into a fight with him. He pulled a gun on me, and I killed him. I was already planning on killing him, so when he pulled his gun out. It was my opening."

"Where are the children?"

"I may have got into a fight over that as well."

"Who with?"

"When I reported this to my boss, he sent someone over to get the kids. The man who came to my house was yelling at them. I couldn't let that happen. When I told him to shut up, he thought he would push me out of his way. So I floored him. He left crying on the phone to his boss. He was from child welfare. After the kids were taken in, it was discovered they were all stolen children. Can you believe that? They were reunited with their families. I was suspended for six months for multiple reasons," she shrugged her shoulders.

"You should have gotten an award for rescuing those kids."

"Yeah, you would think, but I've been staying busy. Skye wanted me to stay with her for a while. Later I figured out she wanted me to help paint her barn."

Kane chuckled. Then he fell silent when he walked into the hospital cafeteria and spotted Bird drinking a cup of coffee sitting at a corner table. He and Julia got their coffee and sat down with her. No one said a word. They drank their coffee quietly. Until Kane raised his head and saw Elie standing in the doorway.

He stood up and hurried to her before she could cry out. He threw his arms around her. "It's okay. Everything is going to be fine. They are with the best surgeons around."

"I should have stayed there. Rory and Jonah are going to die because I left them to go with Austin. What kind of sister am I?"

"You're a good sister. They are not going to die. I need you to stay calm, please. I'm going to get you a cup of coffee. Come with me, and I'll introduce you to Bird. She's Jonah's sister." They made their way to the table. Kane took Elie's hand. Elie, this is Bird, and this is Julia Sparrow. Kane noticed Elie's head swing over and look at Julia. He knew Rory must have told her about when they drank together in Scotland, and Kane told Rory he was in love with a woman named Julia Sparrow.

Bird stood up and hugged Elie, "So you and Rory are identical twins. Did you drive your grandpa crazy?"

"Honestly, we were always too busy to play any tricks. My grandfather would have never been fooled. He was like Kane. He could tell us apart at a glance. We had a grand time growing up until it was time to shear the sheep. Rory would always cry because she claimed the sheep were freezing. I'm sorry I wasn't there to help Rory and Jonah. This probably wouldn't have turned out this way if I had been there."

"IT'S PROBABLY a good thing you weren't. You could have been killed. Rory and Jonah will pull through this. Maybe not in time for their wedding, but maybe they will. I'm going to plan everything as if it's still going to happen. Would you like to help me?"

"Yes, I would like that very much. Thank you."

KANE CHUCKLED, remembering Rory when she was young. "My grandfather made Rory stop helping until she got big enough to know the sheep weren't getting cold."

Julia smiled. "It must have been fun growing up on the farm."

Elie smiled, "It really was. My grandfather was a wonderful man. When our parents and Grandmother died, Grandfather took us in as if we had always lived there. He taught us so many things in life. He would have been ashamed of me for not being there with Rory when those men came." Elie wiped a tear from her cheek.

Kane shook his head, "I'm glad you and Austin weren't there. We might be arranging for a funeral right now. Rory and Jonah will pull through this. They love each other too much to die."

ELIE NODDED. She raised her head when she felt someone watching her. Austin stood over by the counter, looking at their table. I'll be right back," Elie said before standing up and walking to where Austin stood.

As she got closer to him, she could see the pain in his eyes. She knew he blamed himself for not being there to help Jonah and Rory. "Austin, we are not to blame for what happened. It might have been worse if we were there."

"You know that's not true." He took her elbow and walked her out of the cafeteria so the others couldn't see them. "If I would have left you alone, everything would have been fine. I would have been there, and Jonah and I could have handled those men. But because I couldn't keep my hands off of you, I wasn't there. I still can't keep away from you. This is the beginning for us. But right now, I feel responsible for what happened. Stay with your brother, or I swear to God I'll find an empty room and make love to you again. I've never wanted anyone as much as I want you. When everything is back to normal, we'll go away somewhere alone together."

"Austin, I have a sheep farm I have to get back to. I can't take time off just so I can make love to you. I want you right now. Those few hours together weren't enough for me. Find that room and take me there. That's what I need right now. I need for you to take my mind off of my sister and Jonah fighting for their lives."

Austin pulled her as close to his body as she could get. "Do you feel how much I want you?" He whispered into her hair. All he could think about was this beautiful body naked with his. The love they made wasn't like anything he'd had before. His body still had electricity going through it. His lips smashed against hers, only for a moment before he pulled her along with him. He found an empty room and made love to her, and for a while, they forgot to blame themselves for what happened.

19

The doctor walked into the hospital waiting room. Everyone in there jumped up. "Are all of you together?"

"Yes."

"Jonah is in recovery. He lost an awful lot of blood, but his sister donated some, so he now has plenty of blood. I don't have any information on Rory yet. She's still in surgery. The bullet is up against her spine, so we have to be patient. These kinds of surgeries take time. I'll see how it's going and get back to you."

"When can I see Jonah?" Bird asked. Killian had his arm around her so she wouldn't fall apart. Their baby was due in a few weeks, and he worried something would happen to her if Jonah or Rory didn't pull through this.

"They'll be putting him in ICU. You can see him then. Whatever you do when you see him, don't mention Rory. I don't want him upset. His injury took a lot of patching. We had to sew his insides back together. We have to keep him calm. He can't get out of bed."

"I won't upset him, I promise."

"What will you tell him when he asks for his bride to be?"

"I'll think of something. I won't upset Jonah. I'll only stay for a minute."

"Okay, I'm going to trust you. If you have to mention Rory, tell him she's in surgery, and you haven't heard anything."

Bird nodded.

"I'd like to go in with her," Austin said.

"Only two at a time."

Austin walked into ICU with his arm around Bird. When they saw Jonah, he was sleeping, so they never had a chance to talk to him. The sheet was pulled down, leaving his stomach bare. They could see where the surgeon had to repair his stomach, where the bullet did its damage. There was dried blood still on him.

Bird sat in the chair next to the bed and took a deep breath. "Can you ask Killian to come in here and sit with me for a while?"

Austin looked over at Bird. "Are you going to be okay, Bird?"

"Yes, I'm going to stay here with Jonah. Can you let me know when you hear about Rory?"

"Yes, as soon as I hear something, I'll text you."

"Thank you."

~

JULIA SAT NEXT TO KANE, holding his hand. He was glad to have her there. When a man in scrubs walked into the waiting room, they stood up.

"Are you Rory's family?"

"Yes."

"We got the bullet out of her back. It was in a dangerous position near Rory's spine." He shook his head, "We won't know anything until she wakes up. I'm not sure when that will be. She's still unconscious from the injury to her head. So until she opens her eyes, we won't know anything. I tried pricking her feet, but she's in a deep sleep, and there was no reaction. I don't know if she's paralyzed or if she can't feel it because she's still in a coma state. I'm sorry I don't have better news. At least she's alive. We will monitor her brain to see if something is going on that shouldn't be. We'll be taking her to ICU third floor. We can keep a closer watch on her brain there. Only two people at a time can visit her."

"Do you think she has brain damage?" Kane asked.

"We don't know yet. That's what we are monitoring. So don't let the wires bother you. They are there for a reason."

Kane turned and took Elie's hand, "Come on, let's go see our sister." He stopped and looked at Julia, "Will you wait here for me?"

"Yes, I'll be right here."

Marc looked over at Julia, "What's going on with you and Kane?"

"We're friends."

"It looks like you're more than friends."

Julia turned and looked at Marc. "We are friends. I'm here for my friend." Julia went and sat back down. Marc walked out of the room.

KANE AND ELIE walked into the ICU where Rory was. Elie put her hands over her face and cried. She couldn't believe that the young woman lying in that hospital bed was her sister. The surgeon had to cut three or four inches down her back to find the bullet. Her blanket lay across her hips. She was on life support, and her head looked swollen where the bullet cracked her skull.

"Is she even alive?"

"Yes, she is alive. The doctor said she was hooked up to a lot of wires. The wires look bad, but she needs them. They are tracking her brain waves."

"Why is she on life support?"

Kane saw a nurse walk by and stepped up to her. "Can you tell me why Rory is on life support?"

"Are you family?"

"Yes."

"When Rory got here, she wasn't breathing on her own. So her doctor decided to keep her on life support for a couple of days."

"Is she showing any sign of waking up?"

"No, I'm sorry, she isn't. We have all the monitors at our station, so we'll know right away if it shows her brain is doing something."

"Do you think she's brain dead?"

"No, I don't think that at all. When she's ready to wake up, she'll wake up. If you talk to her, I believe that will help."

"Thank you. We'll definitely talk to her." Kane walked back over to Elie, "She said it would help if we talk to Rory."

"Okay, I was already talking to her. Why don't you go see how Jonah is doing?"

"Yeah, I'll be right back. I want to see how Jonah is doing so we can tell Rory when she wakes up. She might have thought Jonah was killed. Maybe that's why she has shut down. If she thinks he's dead, she may not want to live."

"I was thinking the same thing. Kane, go talk to Julia. If you love her, then do whatever you have to do."

"Julia doesn't want to hear I love her. She left when I told her I loved her."

"She's here. That means something."

Kane nodded realizing she had a point. "I'll be back."

Kane heard him before he got to where Bird and Killian were trying to calm Jonah down. The nurse let him in when he told her he was Rory's brother. As soon as he walked into the room, Jonah shut up.

"Tell me, and it better be the truth."

Rory came through her surgery just fine. She hasn't woken up yet. Elie is talking to her. The nurse said that would help. I came to see how you're doing, so I can tell Rory when she wakes up."

Jonah looked into Kane's eyes and knew he was telling the truth. "When I saw those men with those guns, I knew it was going to be horrible. I put Rory behind me, but she wouldn't stay there. When I got shot, I saw her fly past me. I thought I died. Where is she?"

"She's on the third floor."

"Take me."

"No!" Bird demanded. "You listen to me. If you get up, you'll die. What will we tell Rory when she wakes up? 'I'm sorry, Rory, Jonah wanted to see you so bad he went against the doctor's orders, and it killed him.'"

"I'll wait for a couple of days, but if you have to push this bed into her room, you will. I'm going to go to sleep so my body can heal. Rory needs me. What happened to those other men?"

"There was only one the police found him running down the street he had a bullet hole in his side. The others were all dead."

"Rory must have killed them. They weren't all dead when I got shot." Jonah needed to see Rory. He had a feeling she needed him.

"If Rory thought they killed you, she probably freaked out and didn't care if they killed her. So she must have killed them."

"Where was she shot?" Jonah asked Kane.

"In the back and in the head. The bullet to her head didn't penetrate inside, but it cracked her skull. That's why she hasn't woke up. She's kind of like in a coma. They got the bullet out of her back. It was close to her spine, so we won't know if she's paralyzed until she wakes up."

"Oh, God. I need to go to her."

"Tomorrow, I'll come up and push your bed to the third floor. I have to get back up there. I'll see you tomorrow."

Jonah reluctantly agreed, "Okay, I'll see you tomorrow. Kane, will you tell Rory I love her."

"Yes, and I'll tell Rory you are coming to see her tomorrow. I'll see you in the morning."

"Bird, you might as well go home to your children. You look like the baby will be here any minute. I want you to take care of yourself. I'm going to sleep. I'll see you tomorrow."

"Good night, Jonah. I'll go home, don't try going to see Rory on your own."

"I won't." He waited until Bird left before he called Austin. "Are you still in the hospital?"

"Yes. How are you calling me? When I left you a while ago, you could barely hold your eyes open."

"Come to my room. I want your help with something."

"I'll be right there."

"Find yourself some scrubs."

"Scrubs?"

"Yes, you're going to need them."

~

Where the hell am I going to find scrubs? Austin walked the halls until he saw a hospital worker pushing a cleaning cart. He gave his famous cowboy smile that worked on ladies since he was fifteen. "I need to find some scrubs. Can you point me in the right direction?"

"Follow me, and I'll show you where some are kept. Did you forget yours at home?"

He winked and kept the smile on his face. "Yes, I didn't go home last night, so I wasn't able to get mine. I also need some for my colleague. She's afraid she'll be fired if her supervisor sees her not wearing them."

"Yeah, there are some here who let the title supervisor go to their head. Here they are. The size is largest on the top shelf and smallest on the bottom. Good luck sneaking past your supervisor."

"Thank you. I'll change in here." Austin couldn't believe his luck. His flirting smile still worked on the ladies. He hid his clothes in the small room that held scrubs and cleaning material. He found Elie a pair of scrubs and walked as if he worked at the hospital. He went straight to the third floor to recruit Elie to help him with whatever Jonah had in mind.

He lucked out again when he got to the third-floor ICU. The doors had just opened, and a woman walked out. Austin smiled and walked through the doors. He spotted Kane and Elie standing next to Rory's bed. He walked over to them. At first, they paid no attention because of the scrubs. He looked at Rory, and his legs almost gave out on him.

Elie wiped the tears from her face. "Austin, why do you have scrubs on?"

"Here, I have some for you too. Put these on, then we are going to pay Jonah a visit."

"I don't understand," Elie said, taking the scrubs Austin handed to her. Tears still falling from her eyes.

Austin pulled her into his arms and let her cry. He ignored Kane staring a hole through him. "Jonah asked me to get scrubs and go to his room."

"I'll put them on in the bathroom in the hallway." Elie agreed to do it without even blinking.

Kane didn't know if he liked what was about to happen.

He didn't want Elie involved in something that could bring trouble to her. And what the hell was going on with Austin and Elie? He pulled her into his arms like it wasn't the first time she's been there. "What the hell is this about? I already told Jonah I would bring him up here in the morning."

"I don't think he wants to wait until the morning. When we need to come back in, I'll text you to open the doors."

"Alright, but I don't like this. It could cause Jonah damage to his wound."

"We'll be careful with Jonah."

20

Jonah shut his eyes for only a minute. At least that's what he thought. When he opened them again, Austin and Elie sat in the two chairs in his small area in ICU. "What time is it?"

"It's the next day," Austin glanced at his watch, "six in the morning."

"Why didn't you wake me?"

"Because I didn't want to be responsible for you dying by doing something I know might harm you. I think I'm going to regret this anyway."

Jonah looked at Elie, "Elie, how are you doing?"

"I'll be better when Rory wakes up."

"I want you two to take me to Rory. I know if I'm with her, she'll wake up. I can help her. I need to see her. To make sure she's okay."

"She's hooked up to lots of wires, and they have her on life support, but they might take her off today."

"Why is she on life support?"

"She wasn't breathing on her own when she was admitted to the hospital. Her heart stopped as well, but it's working.

So I think when they take her off life support, she'll breathe on her own."

"What are you two doing here? Where are your name tags?" the frowning nurse asked them.

Jonah answered for them, "They are taking me for x-rays."

"I have not seen anything about Mr. Brewer having x-rays. Let me see the paperwork you have."

Elie looked over at Austin. "Do you have the paperwork?"

"No, we must have left them in the janitor's closet when we were in there."

"Why would you be in the janitor's closet?"

Elie looked over at the nurse. "We were changing our clothes."

"Together?"

"Yes, she's my girlfriend."

"Alright, you two, I don't want to hear anymore. Take Jonah where you have to take him but bring him back in thirty minutes."

She took his medication drip tube and hooked it on the bed. Then stood aside for them to push Jonah. She watched as they had no idea how to make the bed move. See these. They are the brakes. You step here, and that will take the brakes off. Then, when you get to where you are going, put the brakes back on." Then she looked at Jonah, "Do not get out of bed."

Jonah nodded. He wasn't about to make himself worse. Jonah knew he had to stay healthy for Rory.

When they got to the third floor, ICU, Austin texted Kane, who came and opened the door. They walked through and right past the nurse's station. They didn't get stopped. In fact, the area next to Rory was cleared, out so they pushed Jonah's bed up next to hers.

Jonah reached out his hand and touched her. "Can you

leave us alone?" he asked, squeezing the bridge of his nose, trying to hide his tears. After everyone left, Jonah put his hand into Rory's. He brought her hand to his mouth and kissed it. He didn't like her color. She had a grayish tint to her skin.

"Rory, sweetheart, will you please wake up for me? I need you to open your eyes, sweetheart. Don't you remember we are getting married in five days? You have a beautiful wedding dress you didn't let me see. I want to see you wearing it at our wedding." Jonah had to pause, tears were flowing down his cheeks. "Rory, I know you were scared when I was shot. You probably thought I had died, but it takes more than one bullet to kill me. If you opened your eyes, you would see I'm almost as good as new. Sweetheart, you are my life. Please wake up. Life isn't worth anything if you aren't here to share it with me. I love you, darling. I will love you until I take my last breath. Now I need you to open your eyes."

The nurse walked into the area and checked the wires on Rory's head. Rory hadn't made any sign that she could hear him.

"When is the doctor taking the life support off of Rory? I think he should do it now. Rory will breathe on her own and wake up sooner. She knows I'm here, but she has to have that life support off so she can talk to me."

"We are taking it off today. As soon as you finish your visit, we'll take it off of her."

"I'll leave for now, but I will be back later today. I'm not staying away from Rory just because I can't get out of bed. Please, if she shows signs of waking up, let me know so I can be here with her."

"You'll be the first to know when that happens. I'll let your friends know they can take you back to your room."

"Thank you." Jonah didn't want to go back to his room,

but he also knew he had to get better before he could help Rory.

~

KANE LOOKED AT JONAH. "What the hell are you doing out of bed?"

"I've been allowed to leave my bed."

"Have you been told you have to be in a wheelchair? I remember hearing them tell you to stay in a wheelchair. I'm sure no one told you it would be alright to walk to visit Rory."

"They didn't tell me I couldn't. It's been a week since we were shot. Today is my wedding day, damn it. I want to spend this day with my wife—" his voice broke, "—so please leave us alone for the entire day."

Kane was tired. He hadn't been eating much. He missed Julia. It probably would have been better if she hadn't shown up. Now, all that pain started all over again. "I'll go and come back tomorrow. I'll tell Elie not to come today. I'm sorry for shouting at you. This just fucking sucks. I can't get any reaction out of her. I promised my grandfather I would keep an eye on Rory. He thought she needed watching over more than Elie, who was more independent."

"You're right. This does fucking suck. I want my Rory back. I understand how you feel. Go take it easy today. I'll be here taking care of Rory. I'll see you tomorrow."

"Yeah, I'll see you tomorrow."

Jonah pulled the curtain close so he could be alone with Rory. "Sweetheart, I know you will be so angry when you wake up and realize you slept through our wedding. Please wake up." Jonah laid down next to Rory. He wrapped his arm around her and kissed her lips. He stayed there for a while, just holding her. Then he got up and did what he did every day. He massaged her legs. Jonah knew Rory couldn't do her daily yoga, so he tried keeping blood pumping in her legs.

"Does that feel good, sweetheart?"

"Oh yeah."

Jonah froze. He shot up and stared at Rory.

"Don't stop."

Her eyes were still shut. "Rory, sweetheart, can you open your eyes?" His voice cracked, but he couldn't help it.

"Why?"

"I want to see those beautiful green eyes of yours. Open your eyes." He was now by her head, touching her hair and whispering to her, "Please open your eyes." A tear fell from his eye hitting her cheek.

Rory tried opening her eyes. "I'm too tired. I can't open them right now."

Jonah held her face in his hands. "Are you awake, or am I dreaming?" he could barely get the words out.

Rory knew something was wrong. She slowly opened her eyes. They gazed into each other's eyes. "You're alive," she whispered as tears spilled over and ran down her neck. "You didn't die."

"No, sweetheart, you saved me," he leaned over and kissed her softly. They were both crying. "You've been asleep for a week. Today is supposed to be our wedding day."

"So why aren't we getting married. I want to marry you. I want to get married today."

"Today? You're barely awake. Are you sure?"

"Yes, I want to marry you today." She was had drifted back to sleep in the next instant.

Jonah looked at the nurse. "Does the hospital have a chaplain who could marry us?"

"Yes, the hospital does have someone who can marry you two. But first, the doctor is on his way up." The nurse turned and looked at Jonah, "Are you supposed to be walking? The nurses on your floor said you were supposed to be in a wheelchair. What if you fall? You could tear all of your stitches out, and we wouldn't know about it until you fell down at our feet. I have a wheelchair coming up. For now, you can sit on that chair over there?" she said, pointing her finger.

Jonah saw Rory's eyes open and panic come over her face. Then, before he could say anything, Rory spoke. "No, please let him stay with me."

"He'll only be right over there. He can hear everything we say. Besides, he's going to call your brother and sister. This is the first time they haven't been here."

"Jonah, just sit on the end of my bed."

The nurse walked over and pushed the chair next to Rory's bed. "There, is that better?"

"Yes, thank you." Rory shut her eyes and was asleep in the next breath.

Jonah's heart fell. He was frantic, "Rory, sweetheart, can you hear me?" He looked at the nurse, "What the hell happened? Why does she keep falling asleep? Rory, wake up."

"You need to calm down. She will wake up again when she's rested more. Did she say anything about her legs?"

"Yes, I was massaging them, and she didn't want me to stop."

"That's fantastic news."

"Did she go back to sleep?" the doctor asked as he walked into the cubical.

"Yes, she didn't seem to have anything wrong with her brain. She also had feelings in her legs. So Jonah is going to call her family. This was to be their wedding day. So they are getting married right here in the hospital today."

The doctor looked over at Jonah. "Are you sure you don't want to wait until she's checked for any paralysis?"

"I don't give a damn what she has. I love Rory. I love her

more than any man could ever love a woman. She is my life." He turned to the nurse who was wiping her eyes, "If you have the information for the hospital chaplain, I'll have my sister call him."

"I'll get it right now." She walked out of the room.

Jonah watched as the doctor pulled out a needle. He was going to stick Rory in the foot. Jonah stepped in front of him. "I told you she had feeling in her legs. So you don't have to prick her."

"If you're going to stay in here while I check Rory, you'll have to sit quietly."

"Jonah, let the doctor check me so we can get busy with our wedding. I wonder if I can wear my gown."

Jonah looked at the doctor.

"Hello Rory, I'm going to see how your body is doing. Are you feeling any pain anywhere?"

"My back is a little tender. But I'm sure with the help of Elie and Bird I can get dressed. Do you have concerns about me being paralyzed? Because you don't have to worry about that, I can feel my entire body. I will have to call Austin as well. I wonder if he's been painting Bird's murals." Rory looked at Jonah, "Did you call Kane?"

Both Jonah and the doctor smiled.

"Yes, sweetheart, they are all on their way back to the hospital. Elie is bringing your dress. All of our friends and family who are close by will be here. When you feel up to it, we'll have a party for all of them." He bent his head and kissed her. "I love you."

"I'm going to be okay, Jonah. You don't have to worry about me. We will have a long, happy marriage with lots of wee babies to keep us busy. Just as we planned. I'm sorry you were so scared when I didn't wake up. It was because I thought you died, and my body shut down. I do notice the bottom of my right foot is tender."

"That's where I pricked you to see if you were paralyzed," the doctor admitted.

There was a lot of noise, then Elie ran into the room and stopped. She started crying and just crumpled on the bed. "I was so scared you wouldn't wake up."

"I'm going to be okay. I woke up, and I can feel my entire body, so I don't want you to be scared anymore." Rory saw Kane standing at the end of her bed. He walked over and hugged her.

"I missed you. I'm glad you're back."

"Me too!"

Elie was straightening Rory's pillow crying the entire time. "Bird is bringing your dress,she took it home to press it yesterday. The chaplain will be here at four-thirty. We are having a wedding. Jonah, go put your tux on. Austin is waiting for you in the hallway."

"Elspeth, stop crying. I'm going to be okay. I'm a little sore, but that's all. Now, smile, it's my wedding day." Rory heard someone walk into her little area. She looked, and Missy stood there. "Missy, did you come for my wedding?"

"No, I came to the hospital because I've been out of the country, and when I got back, in time for your wedding, Polly told me what happened. I'm so glad to see you awake. Did you say you were getting married here?"

"Yes, Jonah and I are getting married here today. You have to stay for it."

"Of course, I will."

21

Rory didn't think she would ever get dressed between Elie and Bird crying and the nurse blowing her nose from her sniffles, trying not to cry. Finally, they had the dress on. Rory was going to be barefoot. She forgot to tell them to grab her shoes.

Kane looked at his sister and had to wipe his eyes again. "You gave all of us a scare. We love you so much. You are so beautiful, Rory. I know our parents and grandparents would be so proud of you."

"Thank you, Kane. I love you too. I think I should hurry and get married. I feel like I'm going to fall asleep. Maybe I'll just sit down on my bed for a minute."

Kane glanced at Rory. Her eyes were closed, and she was sleeping. The family stood around the bed, waiting for Rory to wake up. Jonah smiled at all of them. He touched Rory on the shoulder, "Rory, sweetheart, it's time to get married. Wake up, sweetie."

Rory smiled. "I am awake. I was resting my eyes."

Jonah kissed her then he helped her to stand. "How are you feeling? Are you sure you're up to this?"

"Yes. This is the day we chose, and this is the day that will be our wedding day."

The chaplain walked up to them. "Jonah, can you take Rory's hand in yours. Is there anything either of you want to say to the other before we get started?"

Jonah looked at Rory, "Yes, I want Rory to know she has made me the happiest man on earth by becoming my wife. I will always put you first. I will love you forever. You are the only woman I have loved, and you will be the only woman I ever love."

Rory wiped the tears from her cheeks. She loved hearing Jonah talk with that slow sexy drawl from his southern upbringing. "I love you so much. I want you to know you take my breath away. You always make me feel loved. I'm glad Kane brought me to America, so I could find you. I want to say thank you to my family and my friends for being here to share our wedding day with us." Rory looked around, and her cousin, Callum Walsh, stood in the doorway. She smiled at him. "Now I see my cousin Callum is here to celebrate with us. Which makes it even more of a perfect day."

~

Rory was asleep. Their wedding was perfect. And now Jonah was utterly worn out. He sent everyone home. Callum stayed at his house and helped Austin and Elie finish painting Bird's murals. Thank goodness Rory had already outlined them. Kane had an assignment, so he had to leave. Now all they had to do is get well so they could go home. He crawled in bed with Rory, and they both slept like that for the rest of the night.

Rory woke up early. She opened her eyes to find Jonah watching her. "Good morning, wife. I love you."

"Good morning, husband. I love you so much. I'm hungry.

They took my feeding tube out yesterday. What time do they serve breakfast around here?"

Jonah chuckled, "They want to release me today, and they are putting you in a private room. So I'm going to stay in there with you."

"You don't have to do that. Go home and check on things, get your clothes, and shower. Make sure our garden is taken care of. I don't want you spending your entire day in the hospital with me. You've got too many things to do than sitting here babysitting me."

"I'm not babysitting you. You're my wife. You're my life. I want to spend every day with you."

"I want you to go home and relax, then come back and have dinner with me. But I want you to get some sleep in our bed."

"Okay, sweetheart, I'll go check on things at home. I'll come back for dinner with you. But I'm sleeping here with you."

Rory nodded her head. "Okay, that does sound good." She closed her eyes and went to sleep. When she woke up again, she was in bed alone. She rang for the nurse. "Can I please have a bath?

"Yes, you are also going to another room. I believe the doctor will be releasing you tomorrow."

"Good. I'm ready to go home."

"Did I hear you say you're ready to go home?"

Rory smiled from ear to ear. "You were supposed to come back for dinner."

"I missed you, so I came early."

"I'm so glad you did. I get to go home tomorrow."

"Good, tomorrow is the beginning of our life together. We'll wait about a month before we have our party for our friends and family. Then we'll go to Scotland, and you can show me around."

"That sounds wonderful. Is my cousin Callum still around?"

"Yes, he's with Missy somewhere. I think she took him to Disneyland."

"Good. Who knows, maybe Callum is the one for Missy."

"Now, Rory, don't start matchmaking. Those two live worlds apart."

"I won't do anything. If it doesn't come naturally, then it won't work."

22

Rory was in the barn with Austin. It'd been six months since the shootings. Jonah had an eight-foot wall put up all around the five-acres park-like setting he put up for Rory. Bird's house was finished. She only had one thing left. It was a surprise Rory made for their family. It was something for them to hang on their front porch. She carved a picture of a bird and her husband watching over all their baby birds. Each bird had its name engraved under it. Bird was due at their house in thirty minutes for dinner. Rory would give it to her then.

She looked over at Austin, "Why are you so quiet? You haven't been the same since we came home from the hospital."

"I'm leaving for Texas tomorrow. I'm going to miss you."

"I'm going to miss you too. How long are you going to be there?"

"I don't know yet. I'm not sure if I'm coming back. I've been thinking about becoming a full time rancher. My dad's getting up there in age, and he wants me to live near him."

"What happened between you and Elie? I thought for sure you two had something going on."

"Elspeth lives in Scotland, and I have a ranch in Texas. Our lives are far apart from each other."

"Do you miss her? Is that why you're sad?"

"Who says I'm sad? I'm not sad. I need to be going. I just wanted to tell you goodbye."

Rory hugged him. "I'm sure we'll see you again soon. Jonah and I are going away on our honeymoon. Maybe we'll stop at your ranch on the way home."

"That would be great. I can show you two around. We'll go have some whiskey at the bar there in town."

"You take care of yourself, Austin."

"Where is Austin going?" Jonah asked, walking into the barn.

"He's moving back to Texas."

"What? How long will you be there?"

"I don't know if I'm coming back." They shook hands and did their man hug.

"Thank you for everything. I don't know what I would have done if you weren't here to help. I appreciate everything you've done for us, Austin."

"You're welcome. Goodbye, you two."

They watched him leave. "I thought for sure when I was in the hospital he and Elie had something going."

"I think they did. Both of them have a responsibility to their land and the people who work on it. Those people count on that income. So no matter how much you may want to be somewhere if you have to care for other lives, it's a big responsibility."

"Yeah, I know there are a lot of people who work for Elie. How long are we going to be gone on our honeymoon? Killian's mother wants her bathroom mural painted. I should give her a date."

"We'll be gone a couple of months. I took off the rest of the year so we can travel and have a good time. I would like to have a look at your cousin's castle also. Callum is going to come and watch the house for us. I just talked to him. He's in the United States. I'm not sure where but he'll be here on Monday."

"Have you talked to Kane? I tried calling him to tell him we were going to Scotland, but I couldn't get an answer from him. Elie said Julia came to the hospital to be with him when we were there. I wanted to see how he was feeling about that."

"Are you talking about Julia Sparrow?"

"Yes. I drank some whiskey with Kane when Grandfather died, and Kane came to Scotland, and he spilled the beans. He made me promise never to say a word about it. He was angry, because he told me. He never could hold his whiskey. So don't say anything."

"I kind of figured it out on my own. I was with Kane when he heard about Julia being badly injured once, and he freaked out. I asked him, but he denied it. So I never brought it up again.

So she came to the hospital. She must care for Kane. Skye adopted Julia. Skye was twenty-three, and Julia was sixteen. They are really close."

"I imagine it was hard for Kane when she left again."

"Yeah, I guess it would have been."

Rory shrugged her shoulders. "You never know. It might work out one day for them. I wonder why she wanted to keep it a secret."

"Who knows? Julia works undercover. Sometimes you won't even know she's around, and she'll be standing next to you downtown. Let's not think of them right now. Let's think of us and the fact that it's nap time."

Rory laughed. "Yes, that's the best kind of thinking to do."

23

Jonah, Rory, and Kane stood in the airport. Kane gave them a ride. He said he wanted to tell them goodbye in person. So he volunteered to pick them up and take them to the airport. "Is there anything you want me to tell Elspeth?" Rory asked.

"No, you do know we have phones, right. I talk to Elie at least three times a week. If you want, you can give her a hug for me."

"Okay, I will." Rory saw Kane stiffen and turned her head. There was a beautiful woman with her beautiful blue eyes locked on Kane. Her hair was dark and in a long braid down her back. She walked toward them and stopped in front of Kane,

"Hey, Julia. How are you?" Jonah said, looking from her to Kane.

"Hi, Jonah." She turned her head and gazed into Kane's eyes, "Hello, Kane." Then she looked at Rory, "You must be Rory. I'm happy that you are better." Then she turned back to Kane, "How have you been?"

Kane stepped up to Julia and she took a step back. "I'm doing great."

"How are you, Julia?"

"I'm good. Are you going away?"

"No, I gave Jonah and Rory a ride to the airport."

She nodded. "I'll let you finish your goodbyes." She turned around to leave.

Kane blocked her way. "No, wait. I'll give you a ride home."

"I have my car."

Kane touched her hand. "Can we have dinner?"

"No, I have to go. Goodbye."

"Bye."

Rory thought she would cry from the pain she saw on her brother's face. She wanted to run after that woman and tell her she was crazy. Kane was a great catch. She could see how much she loved Kane. So why was she turning away from that love?

"Kane, go after her. I saw her face. She loves you. Why is she doing this?"

"I don't know." He shook his head. "Hey, you two have a great time. When you go see the castle be sure to walk up to the battlements. You will love it."

Rory hugged him goodbye, and they were on their way. She was sad walking away from her brother. She wanted to help Kane, but she didn't know what to do. Julia wouldn't admit that she was in love with Kane. There was nothing Rory could do.

"Don't worry about Kane and Julia. If Julia doesn't want to be with Kane, there is nothing we can do about it."

"I know, but Kane is such a great catch. She must be stupid. Who wouldn't want Kane?"

Jonah chuckled and kissed his wife. "I agree. He would make someone a great husband. I think Julia is making a mistake. But sweetheart, there is nothing we can do. Maybe they'll get together later when Julia is ready to tell Kane she loves him. But we are going on our honeymoon, and we will not think about sad stuff, only happy things."

"Yes, only happy things. I can't wait to surprise Elie. She's going to be so excited to see us.

~

ELSPETH WAS HAVING a hard time with one of her sheep. She couldn't catch him for shearing. There was no way she was asking one of the others to catch him. They already tried doing everything for her. Instead, she felt the tears falling on her face. She kept her head turned so they wouldn't see her tears. She finally caught him. She dragged him over to where the guys waited for him.

"There, I did it."

Jayden nodded his head. He didn't want Elspeth to start crying again. He heard a vehicle stopping outside of the barn. As he watched, Rory stood at the entrance to the barn. Elspeth didn't see or hear her until Rory, and a man who must be her husband stood right next to her, staring at Elspeth's stomach. Elspeth turned, and that's when she noticed her sister.

"Rory, I'm so happy to see you." She ran over and gave Rory and Jonah a hug. "Why didn't you call me? I could have had someone pick you up. I missed you."

"We missed you too and wanted to surprise you. What have you been doing?"

"It's shearing time. Let's go to the house. I'm going to shower while you show Jonah around."

"Okay," Rory looked at Jonah, who had a big grin on his face. "How are you doing, Elie?"

"I'm doing fabulous. How are you doing? I'm so glad you

could visit. Those stupid tears werefalling again. Rory decided to ignore them.

Rory hugged her again. "I'm doing well. Jonah and I will be walking around the property while you shower. Are you alright?"

"Of course, I'm right as rain. Go take your walk. I'll be right out."

Rory took Jonah's hand. "First, we'll put our suitcases away."

"I can't wait to see your room. Is it all pink and frilly?"

"I don't have pink frilly things." They walked inside, and Rory watched Jonah's face.

"My God, this is amazing. You still have all of their armor. Look at this wood. It's beautiful. How could you leave this behind?"

"Jonah, this is just stuff. You are what's real. I don't care about things. I only want you. We can live in a dumpster, and I wouldn't care as long as you are with me."

Jonah pulled Rory into his arms. "Show me your room."

Rory took his hand and took him upstairs to the top floor. She pushed open her door, and he wrapped his arms around her as he kissed her. He didn't even look around. When he bumped into something, he raised his head and turned a complete circle before whistling. "This is your room."

"It was my room. I'll clean it out before we leave."

"What will you do with all this stuff? I mean, it could be in a museum." He ran his hands on some chainmail that still, to this day, hadn't rusted. He looked around, and those kinds of things were everywhere in this room. The bed itself was the most enormous bed he had ever seen. The wall hangings had to be as old as the property. "Can we take the bed home with us?"

"Yes, we'll send it home with the rest of my things." Rory looked at Jonah. "Did you notice anything about Elie?"

"Like what?"

"Anything. Did you notice anything different?"

"She might have put on some weight, but don't tell her I said anything."

"Oh lord, she's pregnant. Should I ask her about it? Maybe she has a boyfriend. I'll wait for her to tell me she's having a baby. I won't say anything." Rory started putting the clothes in an armoire that was also as old as the house.

"I can't believe Kane didn't want this farm. It's loaded with family history."

"I don't think it had anything to do with family history. I think it had to do with Julia. I believe Kane didn't want to stay away from her."

"You could be right. Let's try the bed out," Jonah said, pulling her over to the bed.

Rory giggled as she helped Jonah pull their clothes off. It was almost an hour before they went back downstairs. They followed the smells from the kitchen. Elie was in there with another woman cooking. Rory ran over and hugged her. "Jonah, I want you to meet Mage. Her family has worked for our family for eight hundred years. Mage, this is my husband, Jonah."

"I'm so happy to meet you, Jonah. Elspeth has told me what a good man ye are. I knew if Rory fell in love with ye that ye had to be a good man."

"Thank you. It's nice to meet you. Something smells wonderful."

"Thank you, it's Rory's favorite food. When I heard she was here, I had to make her favorite food."

"Elie, let me help," Rory said, waiting for her sister to tell her about the baby. Rory was glad she didn't decide to hold her breath until Elie said something to her.

"I'M GOING to have to say something before we leave. It's been three weeks, and Elie's getting bigger. I want to meet her boyfriend and find out if they are in love. Maybe she was rebounding from Austin and she got pregnant. She might not even have a boyfriend. Do you think she fell in love as fast as I fell in love with you?"

"Ask her. That's the only way you will find anything out. Sit down with her." Jonah was looking out the window, and he laughed.

"What's so funny?" Rory asked, looking out the window. Then she laughed. Elie was out there trying to catch a baby lamb who was running in circles. Then Elie fell and landed on her stomach. Both of them ran outside. Elie sat on her butt, laughing.

"Elspeth, what are you doing? Do you want to hurt the baby?"

"What are you talking about?" Elspeth said as Jonah helped her up from the ground. "What's going on with everyone in the States?" Elie tried changing the topic.

Rory shook her head. "Everyone is good. Austin moved back to Texas. He's been different since you left. He seemed sad. I guess he misses you. You should call him."

"Why would I call him? I barely knew him."

Jonah knew that wasn't true. Hell, they were together the entire time she was in the States. They had sex. He stopped thinking and looked at Elie. He would bet a lot of money that the baby belongs to his buddy.

"Okay, I'm having a baby. I had a one-night stand when I was in the States. You two were still in the hospital, and I went to a club by myself." Elie looked at Rory, "You know I can't drink. Well, I drank too many whiskey shots. I woke up in bed with a stranger. I was ashamed of myself. So when I found out I was pregnant, I didn't tell anyone. When you showed up here without notice, I was in shock. I didn't know what to say. Please don't tell another soul. I will tell Kane in my own time."

"My poor sister. I'll stay with you until the baby comes."

"No, this is why I never said anything. I don't want me having a baby to affect anyone else's life. This is my baby and no one else's. I want this baby. When I found out I was pregnant, I was so happy."

"Okay, I would be here with you if you were married. So I really don't know what the difference is."

"I don't want anyone asking why you are here with me and not home with Jonah."

"Call Kane and tell him. I'm not keeping a secret from my brother."

"I will call him tomorrow night. After you two leave for home."

"Call me for anything. You know I'll be here."

"I will. I promise."

"Will you promise to stop chasing the sheep?"

"Yes, until after the baby is born."

~

"JONAH, what are we going to do about my brother and sister? Kane is in love with a woman who doesn't want him to love her even though it's obvious she loves him. My sister is having a baby from a stranger with whom she had a one-night stand."

Jonah wasn't sure about the one night stand, but he would keep that to himself. "We are going to let them take care of their own lives. If they want our help, they know we are here for them. I think we need to work on having our own wee babies."

Rory looked at Jonah. "Are you sure?"

"Yes, I'm sure. I want to have little girls running around our house who look just like their mommy," Jonah said, pulling Rory into his arms and kissing her.

"We have to have little boys who look like their daddy. So we better get started," Rory said, wrapping her legs around Jonah as he picked her up and carried her to their massive bed. "I love you, Jonah Brewer."

"I love you so much, Rory Brewer, and I will until I take my last breath."

THE END

KEEP READING TO FIND OUT WHAT HAPPENS WITH KANE AND JULIA

KANE

Kane was not happy. He'd been lying on his stomach in this damn icy slush for two hours. If the guy didn't show up in the next ten minutes, he was leaving. This entire situation was strange. He had a text on his phone to come here and wait until someone showed up with a kidnapped girl. Kane didn't know who sent the message. He had a feeling it was Julia. He missed Julia, the only woman he's ever loved. The woman who dropped him when he told her he loved her. He had to stop thinking about Julia all the time. He focused on what he was doing. Kane had been staring at the damn cabin like it was going to disappear. He was about to get up and leave when he heard a noise. He held his breath and tried to keep his damn teeth from chattering. It was frigging cold here in the mountains. It sounded like there was a scuffle. Kane looked through the trees and still couldn't see anything. Then he heard a man shouting at someone.

"I told you to shut the fuck up. If you don't stop fighting

me, then I'm going to have to hurt you again. Is that what you want? Why do I always take these damn jobs? I'm not allowed to screw you, but I can beat you. That's pretty damn stupid. I believe I'm going to ignore that order."

Kane watched as he pushed the girl inside the cabin. She fell to the floor. Kane tried standing, and his damn legs were numb from the wet, frozen slush. He did a few leg bends before his legs worked good enough to kick the door open. He could have made a lot of noise and not be heard. The girl was screaming, and the man was swearing. Kane kicked the door open, and the man turned with a knife in his hand. Kane kicked it out of his hand and didn't waste time on the guy. He knocked him out and put zip-ties on his arms and legs. Then he stood up and looked at the girl.

She was a skinny little thing, by what he could see in the dark cabin. She was frightened, and she looked like she was going to make a dash for the door. Kane held his hands up. "I'm here to help you."

"How did you know I was going to be here?"

"I didn't know you were going to be here. I had a text saying a girl is going to need my help. I was given the address, and I've waited a few hours in that icy slush for you to show up. So do you want to tell me what the hell is going on?"

"This man took me from my mother. He shot her and grabbed me." Her chin wobbled. "My father will kill him and his friends for killing my mom and kidnapping me."

"How do you know he has friends?"

"Because they dropped us off at the edge of the forest. They were going to hide the car. We have to hurry and leave. Someone is supposed to come and get me from here. I want my mom back." Tears fell unheeded down her face. "Why did they have to kill her?"

"It'll be alright, lass. I'm here now. Just because your mom was shot doesn't mean she's dead. I've been shot before, and I'm still here. A buddy of mine was shot seven times, and he lived. So keep good thoughts." We need to get the hell out of here. If more are coming back. Do you have shoes?"

"No, they took me from our house, and I didn't have shoes on."

Kane took the boots off of the man and tied them real tight so they wouldn't slip off. Then he took the guy's jacket off. To do that, he had to cut the ties off. Kane worked fast and had the ties back on in a couple of seconds. "Come on, I'll call the police when we are further away from the cabin. Then you can contact your father."

"Okay, I won't let them catch me. I'm not real strong right now. I used to be. But I've been sick."

Kane looked at her. "If you slow down, and if you let me, I can carry you. I don't want these guys catching us. My vehicle is about a mile away."

"I don't care if you carry me. I don't think I can walk or run."

Kane turned and picked her up. "Hang on to me. I'm going to cut through these trees. We need to get as far away from these people as we can. What's your name?"

"Riley."

"Okay, Riley, here we go." Kane ran until he saw lights ahead. They couldn't be hunting for them already. "Don't say a thing. I see some lights up ahead. What kind of vehicle were you in?"

"An SUV. Don't forget someone was going to pick me up from there. So it could be their car."

"That's right. Let me see what I can see." Kane looked at the vehicle as it slowed down. Then they turned the lights out. *Why did they turn out the headlights? Do they know we are out here?* Kane wasn't going to risk Riley's life. He headed for his vehicle. Listening for any noise he could hear. He thought he heard a shout, so he ran the rest of the way to his truck. He put Riley on the passenger side and jumped behind the wheel.

"Call Ryes," Kane said out loud to his vehicle. He could hear the ringing.

"Hello,"

"Rye's, I need your help. I just rescued a girl, her name is Riley. She said the guys who kidnapped her shot her mom. She is going to give you her address." He looked over at Riley while he flew down the back road.

"Hello, Riley, can you give me the information."

"Yes, we live in Malibu. Eight-eight-eight-one-three, Carrigan Road. Can you call my dad also? His phone number is four-two-two five-one-one-three."

"You don't want to call him?"

"I don't think I can. I'm going to be sick." Riley looked at Kane, "Sorry."

"The poor lass started vomiting, then she had the dry heaves. Here lass take this bottle of water and wet this cloth. It'll feel better after you wipe your face off." His car phone rang. "Hello."

"I want to talk to my daughter."

"Daddy," Riley cried.

"Riley, thank God, you're okay."

"They killed mama."

"No, no, honey, your mom is going to be okay. We were so scared for you. Mama wants to say something."

"Riley, are you, okay darling. Did those men hurt you?"

"Mama, I thought they killed you. Tell Daddy those men want to kill him."

"Everything is going to be okay. Here's daddy."

"Riley, I want you to listen to Kane. He's going to help

you. We are all going to a safe house. Kane will bring you to where we are. We'll see you in a little while. We love you, Riley."

"I love you too."

It got real quiet. Kane noticed the lass thinking. She didn't say anything, but he knew she wanted to say something. "What's on your mind?"

"Since I became sick, my parents think we need to live near the hospital. My Dad helped to catch some cartel people, and they must have found him. That's why those men wanted me. I'm sure they wanted to trade me for my dad. This scares me. We've moved three times before I got sick. Now my parents are afraid to move because I've been so sick."

"I'm sorry you've been sick. Can I ask what your sickness is?"

"I had meningitis. I don't have it anymore, so don't worry that you'll catch it. It's taking longer to get well than it should. My parents keep taking me to the hospital to see what's wrong with me. I should be completely healed. But I can't seem to get well."

"How old are you?"

"I'm twenty-two."

"Are you? I would have guessed you were fourteen or fifteen. But then again, I haven't seen you in the light. I'm sorry we have to drive in the dark, but until we get away from this area, we can't have any light."

"Well, since you have only seen me in the dark. I'm ordinary-looking. I don't have any special features. My mouth is too big, and my eyes are goldish colored some time greenish. I do have black eyelashes. I do look younger than twenty-two. My hair is cute," Riley chuckled.

"Now you got me curious."

"Are my parents where I'm going?"

"Yes, they are. We have safe houses all over the United States. I'm not sure which one you and your family will be staying in. If you're tired, you can rest your eyes. We have at least an hour to go."

"Okay, thank you."

24

Kane pulled into one of the six garages at the safe house. When the door closed, a man and woman ran into the garage from the house. The woman was crying, holding her arm that was in a sling. Kane kept the doors locked until he saw Rowan, who nodded his head. When he opened Riley's door, she woke up. Kane smiled as he got his first look at her. She had blue hair and gold-green eyes. She smiled at Kane.

"Hello, Riley."

"Hello, Kane. These are my parents. Jerry and Stephanie Kaiser. Riley's dad pulled her into his arms. I'm so sorry, honey, this was all my fault. I should have hired men to guard you and your mom. I didn't realize how much revenge these men wanted."

"Mama, I thought you were dead."

"No, they shot me in the arm. It must have scared me, and I passed out. When I woke up, you were gone. I freaked out and called your Dad and the police." Stephanie looked at Kane, "How did you know about Rilley?"

"I was having dinner with a lady when I got a text that

said a teenager needed my help. The text told me where to go. It said for me to leave right then. So I apologized to the lady and left. I need to take a shower, and Riley needs to soak in a tub."

Riley looked down at herself, "I don't have any clothes here."

"We'll get you something to wear," Kane said, trying to see where Rowan had taken off to. "Did you see…?"

Before he could finish his sentence, a noise at the back door had him turning with his gun pointed at the love of his life. Too bad she didn't want to admit she loved him too. Instead, she refused to be with him ever again. All because he loved her. Right now, she looked angry. Julia headed straight for Jerry.

"What the fuck is wrong with you. I told you to move your family. Did you not take me seriously? Why didn't you leave?" Julia closed her eyes and counted to three. That's as far as she allowed herself. She looked at the people standing there: the woman, the girl who was actually a young lady, and Kane. She would give anything to still be with Kane. To sleep in his arms whenever she felt like it. It wasn't meant to be. Then she smiled at the young lady. "I'm sorry for yelling at your father. I'm really nothing like that." She heard Kane and Jerry smirk but decided to ignore them. Instead, she focused on Riley, who didn't look well.

She looked at Jerry instead. "So have you decided that's it's to your advantage to go into hiding?"

"Julia, we have gone into hiding. But Riley is sick, and they know it. I believe someone at the hospital is telling them when she comes in, and they followed us home."

"Of course, they did." Julia turned to Riley, "What's wrong with you?"

"I had meningitis. I just haven't been able to get my health back."

Kane took a deep breath, “Can we talk later? I’ve been lying in icy slush for hours. I need a shower, and Riley needs a good soaking. I’ll get you one of my tee-shirts to wear, Riley. Maybe there are some sweats around here that you could put on. I’ll call Austin and see if he knows of any. Damn, he’s been gone a year already. When the hell is he coming back? Follow me, Riley, and I’ll show you where the tub is.” He looked at Jerry, “Did someone tell you where to sleep?”

“Yes, we are all taken care of. Julia, I would like to speak to you.”

“I’m sorry, I don’t have time,” She turned and walked out the back door.

Kane shook his head, “Why are you leaving through the back door?”

“I don’t want to be seen.”

Kane walked upstairs. Even though he had his own home, he’s been staying here most of the time since most of the Seals were married. Four more of his ex-Navy Seal buddies will be here next week. He got a T-shirt for Riley and took it to the room she’ll be staying in. Then he went back to his room and stripped out of his wet clothes. When he stepped under the shower, it felt like heaven. Until Julia’s image popped in his head. He wished he could stop loving her. But she’s the only woman he’s ever loved. He got out of the shower and decided to find something to eat. He missed dinner and was starving. He decided to have a fried ham and egg sandwich. As he cooked his egg, Riley came into the kitchen.

“I bet you are hungry. Neither one of us had dinner. You take this sandwich, and I’ll make another one.”

“Awesome, thank you. I don’t usually eat that much.”

“You need to eat more. That will help you with all the health stuff you have going on right now. I’ll help you.”

"You will? My parents don't say a lot about me eating. I think they are afraid to upset me. They watch me every second. It kind of freaks me out. I want to tell them to stop, but I also don't want to upset them. Thank you for bringing us here. This is the first time in a long time my dad has actually gone to bed."

"Has he left the FBI?"

"He's not FBI. He's DEA. I don't think he's left them. It's just that he's been worried about us, so he hasn't been working much."

"He's DEA? I'll call my friend Lucas tomorrow and let him know what's going on."

"Is that Lucas Ryan?"

"Yeah, do you know him?"

"Yes, I haven't seen him since I was about sixteen. He always seemed angry to me. He's my Dad's friend."

"He used to be angry all the time. Until he married Skye. Now he's happy. Did you like your sandwich?"

Riley looked at her plate, and the sandwich was gone. She laughed. "It was delicious."

Kane gave her another one. "Are you still in school?"

"Yes, I'm a senior in college; I've been doing my school on the internet. I need to get my computer and some things from my house."

"We'll worry about that tomorrow. I'm sure your house is being watched. I'm going to head up to bed. Make yourself at home here. But don't go outside. The alarms are crazy loud."

"Okay, thank you."

KANE WALKED UPSTAIRS THINKING about Julia. If he could go back he never would have told Julia he loved her. He knew she had strong feelings for him when Rory, his sister, was in the hospital, and they didn't know if she would live or not. Julia came to the hospital to be with him. She stayed there until the doctor said Rory would live. Julia said nothing to him about the two of them, and he wasn't allowed to say anything to her about them. Their love was hidden from everyone while they were together. Julia didn't want anyone to know they were in a relationship. So for the six months, they dated he never told his friends, and Julia never told her friends. A couple of his buddies knew he didn't know how they found out, and he didn't care. The only ones who knew were his sisters. When his grandfather died, he went back to Scotland. He and Rory had a few shots of whiskey together. Rory could drink almost anyone under the table. Kane spilled his guts after a few shots of whiskey and some perfectly timed questions from Rory. Then she had to tell their sister Elspeth he was in love with someone named Julia Sparrow.

Kane took a cold shower and went to bed. He was damn tired. This was a long day, and to see Julia at the end of it shook him up. He did wonder why the cartel was after Jerry Kaiser. They might have to put them in a different safe house. They would all decide tomorrow morning at the meeting they were having.

25

Kane could smell coffee and bacon as he came down the stairs. Someone was cooking breakfast. He walked into the kitchen, and his sister Rory was cooking. "Why are you here this early?"

"Jonah had lawyer stuff to do, so I came with him to visit you. I knew the way to get you downstairs was to cook breakfast."

"You look happy. What's that smile for?"

Rory set the spatula down and turned to Kane. "I'm having a baby. Can you believe I'm going to be a mother?"

Kane picked her up and swung her around. You're going to be a wonderful mom. I'm so happy for you."

"Thank you. I am so happy." Rory turned back to the stove and saw a movement. "Hello."

"Hi."

"Riley, this is my sister Rory. She just told me I'm going to be an uncle."

"Congratulations."

"Thank you," Rory said. Come over here and take a chair. I have breakfast ready for you."

Riley sat down. "I don't usually eat breakfast."

"Oh, that would hurt my feelings if you don't eat at least a little."

Kane was already digging in. He looked at Riley. "You don't want to hurt Rory's feelings. She's pregnant. She may start crying."

"I'm sorry, of course, I'll eat. It looks delicious."

"It is," Kane said, handing her a biscuit slathered with butter and honey.

He smiled at Rory when Riley ate that biscuit and took another one, and slathered it with butter and honey herself. Rory got up and poured Riley a glass of orange juice. Help yourself to some more. I always cook way too much."

"This is delicious. I could listen to you and Kane talk forever. It makes me want to go to Scotland, and I've never been there."

"Oh, you have to go. It's beautiful everything is so green. I miss taking long walks. I used to walk everywhere I went. My husband had the land behind our house landscaped like my homeland. Everything is green."

"One day, I will go. I promise that's one country I will visit." Riley looked at Kane. "I have class this morning. Would it be alright if I go and get some of my things?"

"You can't leave here. But we'll get your things as soon as everyone is up. Why are they not up?"

"They left," Rory said, taking a drink of her orange juice.

"What do you mean? Who left?"

"Rowan took Riley's parents to another safe house."

"Are they wanting Kane to take me to them?"

"Kane will have to call Rowan. I have no idea what they are doing."

Kane took out his phone. "Hey, Rowan, where are you taking Riley's parents?"

"We are going to separate them. When Riley needs to go

to the hospital, one of us will take her. But from now on, she'll go to a different hospital."

"I think that's a good idea. I'll let Riley know what's going on. She needs her computer for school and her clothes."

"Ryes and Julia went over there. They should be back where you are any time."

"Why is Julia involved in this?"

"Because this was her case. The cartel found out Jerry was a DEA and went after him. Julia warned him three times to move away. He moved, and you know the story from there. Frankie is coming over this morning to check Riley."

"Okay, who is going to guard Jerry and Stephanie?"

"Luke Wilson is with them. Hunter Brown is on his way there. I'm going home. I'll talk to you later."

"Okay, I'll talk to you later." Kane looked at Riley. "Your parents are at another safe house. You'll stay here with us. Julia and Ryes have gone to your house and are packing your things and bringing them here."

"So my parents aren't going to be here with me?"

"No, does that bother you?"

"No, I know I'm going to sound ungrateful for them taking such good care of me while I've been sick. But both of them smother me. I feel like they watch every breath I take. My mom and dad are so scared I'm going to die. Does that sound mean?"

"Not at all."

"Did your parents smother you?" First, she looked at Kane, then Rory.

Kane shook his head. "No, our parents died in an accident along with our grandmother when we were young. Our wonderful grandfather raised us."

"I'm sorry."

"We had a great life growing up. No reason to be sorry."

Kane heard the garage door closing. "I think Julia and Ryes are here." Ryes walked in carrying two suitcases.

"Hello, these must belong to you." He looked at the table, "Is there any breakfast left?"

"Yes, I put the food in the oven."

"Thank you, Rory. I swear you are the best cook."

Kane chuckled, "That's what you told me."

Riley giggled and stood up. "Both of you are great cooks." She looked at Ryes, "Thank you for getting these things for me. Is my computer in here also?"

"No, I have your computer right here," Julia said, walking into the kitchen carrying two bags.

Julia stopped as she saw Riley wearing Kane's T-shirt. She knew it was his. She's taken it off of him before. Pain slammed into her heart, and water rushed to her eyes. *What the hell is the matter with me? This poor girl is sick. Why am I jealous? I'm the one who stopped this relationship with Kane. I had no choice. Everyone who ever loved me has died. I will not be responsible for the man I love dying.*

Kane saw the pain cross Julia's face. "Julia, are you alright?"

"What? Yes, I'm alright. Here you go, Riley. How are you feeling?"

"I actually feel much better. Thank you both for getting my things for me. Now I have to get to class." Ryes followed her, carrying her bags.

Kane turned to Julia. She blinked her eyes to get rid of the moisture. "Rory, this is Julia Sparrow. Julia, this is my sister Rory."

"Hello, Julia."

"Hi, Rory. I'm so happy you are better. Kane was very worried."

"Thank you. I know he was. I'll try to stay away from flying bullets." Rory thought neither of them heard her.

"Well, if you will excuse me, I'm going to call Jonah and see what time he's picking me up," Rory said, stepping away from the table.

"It was just Kane and Julia standing in the kitchen. "Julia,"

"Yes."

"Can we please talk?"

"I have to leave. I have to contact Juan in two hours."

"Juan, are you talking about frigging cartel Juan?"

"Yes."

"When are you going to stop trying to kill yourself? You told me two years ago you would stop taking on these assignments."

"I know these people. Should I let someone who doesn't know anything about the cartel do my job? Someone who could get killed for not knowing if they were saying the right thing? I know these people, Kane. They know me. To them, I'm Sonya Skittle. Someone who knows what she's doing. They trust me. I don't want to be responsible for a newbie dying again."

"You can't take care of every new FBI agent."

"Kane, I did leave. Just like I said I would. Mike Harris was sent in. He was undercover. He lasted three days. Three fucking days before they killed him. So what would you have me do?"

"Send a seasoned man in. It doesn't have to be a new agent. You promised me you would quit. Just because you no longer wanted us to be together doesn't mean you can break a promise."

"I didn't say I wanted us to be apart. I said we had to because you said you loved me."

"So, are you saying if I take back the, I love you part, then we can start seeing each other again?"

"Do you still love me?"

"Do you love me?"

"I have to go." Julia grabbed a biscuit off the table and turned around. Kane caught her arm. He turned her to face him.

He leaned his forehead to hers. "I wish like hell I didn't love you, but I do." Then he held her face in both his hands and kissed her like he knew it would be their last kiss. Kane knew Julia had some issues about loving anyone. "How can I just turn off my feelings?"

"I don't know." Julia stepped back and turned around and left."

Rory wiped her eyes, "I'm sorry I overheard your conversation. I was afraid if I moved, then Julia would hurry and leave before you were finished talking. I wonder why she's so scared to let someone love her."

"So, you think Julia's afraid of me loving her? That could be true, but I can't take it back. I do love her. I'm not going to lie and tell her I don't."

"No, you can't do that. You should talk to Skye. She adopted Julia when she was sixteen. I think Skye was twenty-three when she adopted some teenage girls. That's been some years back now. She probably knows her better than anyone."

"Yeah, I'll give her a call and see if I can talk to her. I better go check on Riley."

"She's doing school work. I was just in there. Thank God you got to her in time. How did you know where she was?"

"I got a text. I'm sure it was Julia who sent me the text." So I will have two nieces or a niece and a nephew. Speaking of nieces, have you talked to Elie lately?"

"I tried calling her this morning to tell her about the baby. But she must have been busy. I'll call her tonight."

"Hey sweetheart, how's my little mommy?" Jonah said as he walked up to Rory and kissed her. And kissed her, and kissed her.

"You know when the baby's here, you'll have to do most of your kissing in the bedroom?" Kane said, grinning.

"Bull, our baby is going to know how much we love each other. I'll kiss my sweetheart as often as I can. Are you ready, sweetheart?"

"Yes, I want to finish the baby's bed and dresser. We won't paint it until we know what we are having. I'm so excited."

"I'm excited too, darling." Jonah wiped a tear from her cheek. "Are you going to cry the entire nine months?"

"Probably."

Kane thought his eyes might water, watching his sister. She was so happy. "I'm glad you got to come by and visit. Let me know if you talk to Elie."

"I will. I love you. When you have a few days off, come and stay with us. I miss you."

"I will. I'll call you as soon as I get some time off."

KANE

HTTPS://WWW.AMAZON.COM/DP/B097FCYX1R

Thank you, for reading my book. If you enjoyed it can you please leave me a review?

FOLLOW ME ON SOCIAL MEDIA

Newsletter Sign Up http://bit.ly/SusieMcIver_Newsletter

Facebook Page: www.facebook.com/SusieMcIverAuthor/

Facebook Group: www.facebook.com/groups/SusieMcIverAuthor/

https://www.bookbub.com/profile/susie-mciver

https://www.susiemciver.com/
https://www.instagram.com/susiemciverauthor/
ZANE BOOK 3
My Book

STORM BOOK 4
https://www.amazon.com/dp/B08Y7C9D4Z

JONAH BOOK 6
My Book
ASH BOOK 5
My Book

ROWAN BOOK 2
My Book

KILLIAN BOOK 1
My Book

Milton Keynes UK
Ingram Content Group UK Ltd.
UKHW020150030124
435363UK00016B/1527

9 781737 575559